The Bicycle Messenger

Linda Conn-Amstutz

The Bicycle Messenger

Linda Conn Amstutz

Front cover photograph by Debbra Obertanec of
Shadetree Photography.

Dedication

To Nancy and Tony Roberts who opened the world to me.

Chapter ONE

Spring 1941, Thursday evening,

Liège Belgium

I was not included in this evening's dinner. That in itself seemed rather odd. I've been allowed to join my parent's dinner parties for well over a year. I think my parents like showing off my excellent manners and perhaps even my beautiful clothes. Mama said she is very proud of the young lady I have become and Papa called me his little jewel...but not tonight.

They have been entertaining Papa's biggest competitor. He had not been invited before to our home but now seems to be an honoured guest. Cook worked feverishly to prepare the most elegant of meals from what she was able to get from her friends that Papa says are "somewhat unsavoury and very expensive, but useful" and the best wine had been selected from Papa's cellar. The evening went on for a very long time and I became more and more curious as it progressed. When I could stand it no longer I tiptoed out of my bedchamber to the top of the staircase just as Herr Schmitt was taking his leave. To my surprise Papa embraced him as he would a dear friend and handed to him the large brass key which I recognised as the key to our gallery. Papa deals in antique art and collectibles, and he just gave his fiercest rival the key to his shop! Perhaps I had not understood their relationship at all. I was going to have to ask Papa about this as I am sure he would want me to understand…

* * * *

Spring 1941, Friday very early morning,

Liège, Belgium

I awoke to find Mama, a candle in her hand, in my bedchamber.

She seemed unnaturally calm but her hands trembled as she chose just a few clothes to pack into my very smallest valise.

"Where are we going, Mama?" I asked her, but she quite rudely shushed me and continued folding and then refolding my underthings.

She has told me not to use such rude and thoughtless sounds as "Shhhh!" It was much more polite to say "Just a moment, please."

Something was very wrong.

The door slammed below in the entry and I heard voices but not the words. Then my mama ran (she never runs) to the top of the stairs then back to my room, where she picked up her own valise and mine in her hands.

"Come, sweetheart, we must go ...NOW!"

"Where, mama? May I bring Sascha? Can we not have breakfast before we leave? I'm hungry."

"No! Sascha must stay here with the servants, you come NOW!" She was nearly screaming, her voice shrill with anxiety as she took my precious puppy from my hands and put her (rather roughly) on the settee.

"We are going for a little trip. I will explain it later when we are safely on the train; for now we must make haste! Come, just put this dress on over your nightclothes and hurry!"

I did as she asked, and we were quickly away from the house with only the least possible luggage. It must be a short trip...and me with my nightie under my dress...how odd!

We made the trip to the station in an unfamiliar car with a driver I had not seen before. Papa said it belonged to a friend who had lent it to us just for this short trip. Herr Schmitt perhaps? Stranger still.

If I had thought the packing and the ride to the station odd, when we arrived it got odder still. In the back of the borrowed car was, in addition to our three small valises, a trunk. It was the sort we took for a very long trip. When Papa and the driver lifted it from the car it seemed weightless. The men carried it to the space where the trains come, and the driver vanished.

There were all sorts of people on the platform, not all first class passengers – some had very soiled clothing and some smelled not very good. Others had no luggage at all but the thing that was the same about all of us was a look of fear and strangeness, as if none of us knew what was going to happen next.

Certainly, I did not.

Finally a train came. The placard on the side of it said "Bordeaux" – that, I knew from my tutor, was in the southwest of France. It would be a very long journey for so few clothes and when I tried to ask, my mama shushed me once more! I was, by then and in spite of both my parents' assurances that all was well, getting very worried.

I was twelve years old and mostly my parents treated me with respect. They usually spoke to me in an adult manner as my age would recommend. This day, however, I might as well have been three years old and not respected at all!

We clambered aboard the train amidst much pushing and shoving and some language I preferred not to understand. We finally found a compartment but had to share it with an older couple in rather shabby attire. They spoke a language that I did not know.

We rode for a while and, sitting up between my parents, I slept, since I'd been awakened in the middle of the night. The train stopped and started, briefly rousing me from my sleep. It was dark and then light, then dark again. Once, the train stayed motionless for a very long time. I awoke but kept my eyes closed thinking I might hear some conversation that could explain our unusual circumstances.

Papa said "We should change trains in Poitiers" (where?) "and go as far as we can to the south. After Limoges there was a man with sandwiches and we shared some – Papa traded a small silver tray for them. He said to Mama, "There is but one thing left to trade besides your earrings, the Madonna." That was all I heard.

We eventually got off that train and Papa and Mama had to drag the cumbersome trunk themselves, as no servants were there. I carried all three of our valises.

I asked Papa "Are we going to Bordeaux? Why did we change trains? Papa…" He told me to "Hush." Was I to learn nothing?

We then took another train after quite a long wait and shortly after arrived at a small town. I saw the signs as we came into the station: "SIORAC"

It was a very tiny train station but quite pretty.

There was no one on the platform when the train arrived but a Catholic priest, and my parents were whispering to each other as they looked out of the train window as we slowly entered the station. Then suddenly, around the corner came German soldiers - probably 8 or 10 of them in brown uniforms and they were armed!

Quickly, before I knew what was happening Papa lifted me and stuffed me into the big empty trunk while Mama made whimpering noises. Papa put a small parcel into my hands, saying, "Sell this, if you need to, to escape France. Go to Spain if you can; do not let the German soldiers see you and do not lose this.

"You must be very quiet, the priest will help you.

"Do not make a sound.

"Your Mama and I love you more than anything in the world, believe this forever. We love you, always."

"I...l-l-love you too..." I tried to say but it was too late.

He had shut the trunk and I felt it (and me!) being trundled off the train and – I supposed – onto the platform.

I heard some German words, then a French man's voice protesting "No, that trunk belongs to me, it is church property, you must not interfere with church property!" followed by muffled grunts and groans and then...nothing.

I stayed quiet for what seemed hours. I am a very good girl and when I am told to keep quiet, I do keep quiet.

So I kept silent for what seemed like forever. I heard nothing after the puff, puff, puff of the train leaving the station. Were my parents on the train? Why had they left me in the trunk? How long must I be so quiet? I was confused, but mostly I was frightened. I was very frightened.

I was also hungry, it was very musty smelling in the trunk and small, my neck hurt and I needed the toilet.

Just when I thought I could wait no longer I heard footsteps on the platform and the clasp of the trunk was rattled. Then there was light through a crack and the trunk was opened.

The priest I had seen earlier peered into the opening and said, "Hello there, I'm *Père* Joseph. And you are?"

"A-Annaliesa," I answered; it was all I could manage.

"Please, come with me. You will be safe soon enough. I am here to help you."

"I need to find a toilet."

"Can you wait just a bit? It would be best to be gone from here." His voice carried a real sense of urgency.

I was not sure I could, but I nodded and followed him as he walked very quickly off the platform and across the road and into the church on the other side. I was still clutching the packet my Papa had given me, but I had no other belongings…not my valise, nothing at all, only the packet.

Père Joseph seemed a serious but kindly man with a mostly bald head fringed with reddish fuzz, and after he had shown me the facilities I needed he took me to a room in the back of the church and brought me a bowl of perhaps the most wonderful soup I'd ever tasted. Or maybe it was just that I had had nothing to eat since…I couldn't remember…yesterday?

After I had finished the soup, he showed me a settee and said "You can sleep here, you'll be fine and no one will disturb you. Here is a blanket - do you think you'll be warm enough? I nodded. The blanket smelled a bit stinky but was warm and I was very tired, or I just wanted to close my eyes and shut out the world for a while. It seems to be a world I don't understand and don't want to be in.

He said, "Tomorrow we will try to get you passage to Spain. Sleep now, you are safe here."

"Where are my parents? Will they come with me to Spain?"

"*No, petit chou*. They have gone to work in Germany. I think they will be there a while. You sleep now."

And I did. I was alone, without those I love and who love me, in a strange country but I went to sleep and I escaped it all.

---

* * * *

Spring 1941, Sunday morning,

The village of Langnac in Southwest France

The stiff-spined, blond, bespectacled soldier of the Third Reich walked briskly past the crowded church-yard, barely glancing in the direction of the parish-ioners. But he was there – he, or one of his kind, seemed always to be there.

The grown-ups continued talking as though he weren't, but they were deeply and painfully aware of his presence and of the danger that presence brought. The hatred of these villagers and farmers, fresh from mass, toward the German soldiers did not seem con-vergent with their recently evidenced Christian faith.

Three village boys, all about eleven years old, looked furtively from behind their parents who stood in a knot, gossiping and making plans for the planting, much of which would take place the following week. Germans or no, the maize and oats must be planted.

The tallest boy, the one with sandy hair and freckles, jerked his head to the left – toward the bushes where his bicycle was "parked" – and the three moved as a single organism in that direction. They were one in purpose, and neither the Germans nor their parents' neighbors would stop them...or even, they hoped, be aware of their aim that day. The two darker boys, one limping slightly, whispered to each other "Is anyone looking?" then "No, I don't think so." and then, as if it were choreographed, all three stopped. The old bicycle lying on its side against the bush was a rusted and sad looking thing, but it had been oiled where oil should go and it worked; though not silently – not silently at all. There was only one rubber grip on the handlebars. The other was long since gone – maybe to the same place as the missing pieces of seat cover and the entire rear fender.

The sandy-haired boy hoisted the bicycle up. Meanwhile, the other two boys stood together – effectively creating a barrier between the after-mass crowd, the German and the bicycle. Swiftly, he slipped something into the handlebar with no grip and gracefully swung his leg over the seat. Waving to his friends and laughing, he turned into the lane toward the nearby village of Siorac. On his ride he crossed the boundary between his friends' town--seemingly overrun, if not formally occupied, by the German army, and his home. He flew through the checkpoint without so much as a wave at the soldiers and into Vichy France, governed by the régime of Marshal Petain. Eventually, he reached the hamlet where his parents lived and where their barn hid the girl with the dark eyes.

Linda Conn Amstutz

Chapter TWO

September 5, 1995

Air France Flight 47, Seat 18 F, Newark, NJ to Paris

Will I never get this right? I've been scrambling for a week--attending to seemingly endless details at the office and then, at the last minute, cramming my suitcase full of clothing and books for my annual month-long stay in rural France. Now that I am finally in my seat on the plane, I wait for that chilling moment when I remember what indispensable thing it is I have forgotten in all the rush!

Got the tickets, passport, a few euros, and a credit card. This is good. The other passengers around me are finally getting settled and…

My cell phone rings. Why didn't I turn the damned thing off before I got on the plane?

It is probably the office, one last thing… Why didn't I turn the damned thing off before I got on the plane? They will handle things well while I am gone - if I just let them do it! God! It will be good to be shed of this responsibility for a while.

Nope, it's John.

"Do you miss me yet?" he said, mimicking cheerfulness.

"I actually haven't had time to notice you're not here!" I said callously. "But I'm sure, as soon as I do, I'll miss you like crazy…" Trying to back down and not sound like such a shrew, I add, "Gotta go; they're closing the doors to the plane. See you in a month!" The doors are closed.

No more cellphone. I switch it off – for an entire month! It won't work in Europe and I am actually glad. None of that pressure for four weeks!

Chapter THREE

September 5, 1995

On the Way

We are taxiing now. It feels like we are driving to Paris. When will they get this plane in the air? My favorite part of the flight is the feeling of being pushed back in my seat just as we leave the ground.

As I said, I have my passport and that much is good. I have a credit card – so if I have forgotten something really vital I can buy it. So what am I worried about? It is just the habit of being stressed, I guess. This is a habit I am on the verge of NOT having anymore.

Whatever in the world will I do with my mind if I don't have the agency to worry about? Twenty years in the advertising business has formed some habits which are surely going to be hard to break – but it seems to be time to begin breaking them.

---

* * * *

Having reached our cruising altitude, the flight attendant comes by, touches my shoulder to rouse me from my thoughts and asks, "Would you like something to drink, *Madame*?"

"Vin blanc, si'l vous plait," I answer. I may as well get started trying to speak French – at least to the extent that I can. My fifty-year-old brain seems to be too old to handily learn a new language, but on the last two visits to France I hired a tutor to at least keep my embarrassment at knowing only one language to a minimum.

Several years ago, three friends and I were driving around and tasting wine on vacation in a tiny town in

Pommerol in the Bordeaux region of southwestern France – what was it, five years ago? We saw a "*Degustation*" (tasting) sign in front of a house on a side street and stopped our rental car in the driveway. A slightly bent-over old woman with tightly curled white hair and a lace collar on her dark dress led us from her back door into her dining room where she had four bottles opened for tasting on her dinner table. The tablecloth probably had belonged to (was crocheted by?) her mother or grandmother. It looked hand-done and had the golden hue of age plus some spots of experience with the wonderful red wines of this region. She poured us some of each vintage so that we could choose which we might want to buy. There was an offering from 1982, 1984, 1986 and 1987 – all *Chateau la Violette*, her family's winery.

We tasted and talked among ourselves – my three friends and I, as she was only speaking French and we were only able to speak English. It was painful, but eventually we accomplished what we needed to without a common language. We made our choice after a friendly argument shortened only by the fact we were hungry and thirsty and ready to get on with lunch waiting in the car. We had fresh crusty bread, a *Camembert* and some pears - needing only this last addition to make the perfect picnic. So we bought four bottles of the 1987: two to share for today and one for each couple to carry home.

The dickering began. The old woman took a small pad of scrap paper stapled together in one corner and began to write numbers; she'd done this before. Finally, we agreed. She smiled and disappeared for a few moments before she came back with four bottles of the 1987. We pooled our resources and came up with enough cash. This was not a place where a credit card was likely to be accepted. She took the francs and we took our wine and walked toward the door when she said to us – in nearly <u>unaccented ENGLISH</u> – "...and next year you will come back and we will do this <u>in FRENCH</u>!" And she laughed.

This has always been the best example I can think of why I <u>need</u> to learn French. I come every year to this part of the world for a month of rest and reconstitution, and the French seem tolerant - to a point – but the four of us had stood in this old woman's dining room in _her_ home in _her_ country and spoken a foreign language to her and expected her somehow to understand. It embarrasses me still.

Time for a nap. It has usually been easy for me, whether it is the _vin blanc_ or the sound of the jet's engines or the fact that preparation for a month-long absence from work and home leave little time for sleep the week prior to departure. Who knows? But the long transatlantic portion of the flight has, for me, gone quickly.

I'm soon shuffling, sandy-eyed, along toward the baggage claim in _Aeroport Charles de Gaulle_. Then, loaded down with my luggage, through Customs and toward the train station, which has only recently been added to the airport.

A very fast train trip (and another little nap on the way) gets me to the station in Bordeaux.

On arrival, I joyfully receive the traditional two _bisous_ (cheek kisses) from my dear friend Clare who, though she is an American, has made France her home for nearly twenty years. Clare who is a fierce hugger said " I'm soooo happy to see you Marg! How was the flight? Have you eaten? Do you need the restroom before we start? Oh! I'm SO glad you're here!"

Clare is both my friend and my landlady – she rents me a small house on her hilltop farm just outside the village of Langnac in southwestern France.

Langnac's an hour by car from Bordeaux on a series of roads most of which are barely wide enough for two small European cars to pass each other. The road follows the circuitous paths taken by some medieval Gallic farmer's cows. As the crow flies - well, never mind – even the crows take indirect routes here. It is part of the charm of the French countryside.

Clare begins, "You'll be amazed by Rachell's baby… a proper little boy now, Henri, he's two. And the field behind your *pigeonnier* is, well, was in sunflowers, but now it's just stubble. I have a couple of photos so you can see how nice it looked. Are you still seeing that preacher? What was his name?"

"His name is John and, yes, I am. He's really very nice…"

Clare interrupts, "Nice, but what?"

"Oh, you know, he's getting pretty intense."

"Oh, dear. Not a good time for you with the sale of the business and all."

Once we arrive at *Bellevue* – her aptly named home perched on the top of the hill – Clare rumbles her little car up over the bumpy grass of the meadow right to the door of my pigeonnier. "There, she says, you won't have to schlep that heavy case up from the lane! You'll have just enough time to unpack before supper."

And I think "Perhaps finally figure out what, in my haste, I have forgotten!"

Clare adds "Be down at my house in half an hour and I have a surprise for you! My neighbor Jean is coming to join us!"

The airline has fed me dinner and breakfast and I had a crusty sandwich of ham and butter on the train – so I don't need much to eat but Clare's company is good and it keeps me from falling directly into bed before dark and getting my circadian rhythms irrevocably out of whack. This will be interesting, I haven't met this "Jean," and all Clare told me was that she had a

new neighbour...but she smiled and...was she blush-
ing?

Chapter FOUR

September 6, 1995

Bellevue near Langnac, France

I love almost everything about this place. One of the best things is how much the same it stays from year to year. I am nearly the only "tenant" Clare has and so the house stays exactly as I left it eleven months ago. In the beginning, when Clare and Peter first renovated this former *pigeonnier* (pigeon coop) they worked at marketing this place as an idyllic mini-vacation venue, then Clare's books, published first in England, became popular and Peter...left. Since she was no longer dependent upon the cash created by renting it, Clare was mostly relieved not to have to launder sheets and towels and sweep up after tenants. One tenant, however, persisted – me.

Picture this: the building is about 30 feet square. It is built of limestone. Square or rectangular sawn blocks of it stacked for the corners and stones gathered from surrounding fields and a bit of rubble make up the rest of the walls. I don't have anything to base this on but guesswork, but I think the builders put up wooden frames and filled them with the stones from corner to corner then poured the mud down through the rubble to "glue" it together. At least thats the way it looks to me…and the amazing thing is; it is still standing! After centuries!

My *pigeonnier* has two floors now but originally it was simply a tower and the lair of a nocturnal carnivore. On the beam that crosses from the front wall to the back one evidence could be seen of a large owl (in white streaks) the detritus from his breakfasts, lunches and dinners in the form of small animal skeletons littered the bare dirt floor. On that, my first, visit there was but one opening through which light could pass - but now after the renovation there is a front door with nine panes of glass, and on the opposite wall, a French window where the old entrance had been. Upstairs, Peter and Clare added a mezzanine floor and a large window overlooking the glorious and ever-changing view of the valley. An undulating field one year of corn, sunflowers or wheat the next, flows down to the lane running past the very active farm of M. and Mme. Jaubert.

Back in the times of the Signeur and his serfs, the landlord was the only one legally allowed to take game. It was a hanging offense for anyone else. There was a loophole, however. If a pigeon was inside your "house" it was "fair game" so these pigeon-friendly towers popped up all over! There are a couple of small pigeon shaped holes on each face of the tower just under the roofline and places for pigeons to comfortably and safely roost inside... et voila! A *pigeonnier!* The farmer's family must have eaten well (at least until this owl took up residence).

Clare and Peter first civilised their own house (the original farmhouse) and that took quite a bit of doing. When they got off the train in Langnac Claire suggested they stop and buy a mop and bucket, etc., to begin cleaning the floors of their new home, which Peter had seen, but she hadn't. He wisely postponed the cleaning purchases because, what he knew and she didn't was that there basically was no floor to mop... some rotted boards were strewn across the damp earth inside the front door. First they must mend the roof then put in a floor and then they could mop.

They did little else for the better part of two years and shortly after the "privy burning party" to celebrate the civilising of their farmhouse, I came for my first visit. I slept, in those days, in their spare bedroom. Soon they began work on the *pigeonnier* and the skills they'd honed working on their house served them well and the fact that this was a much smaller building meant that within a year, in fact in time for my next visit, it was ready for habitation! They knocked out stones for the front door and the upstairs window and built the mezzanine floor (after installing an oak beam to support it) and plumbed the bathroom (upstairs) and kitchen (downstairs). Peter told me the hardest part was putting proper grout in the place ("pointing" he called it) of the mud betwcen the stones in the downstairs walls. After that experience the upstairs walls got a nice even coat of plaster! The atmosphere of warmth created by the natural stones gathered from the fields surrounding the place was worth all the aching wrists he had to endure in the process - of course, they weren't MY aching wrists.

I never thought much about the others who rented this place, it has always seemed like my *pigeonnier*. And it is my *pigeonnier*; at least for this month it is!

The open shelves above the sink hold the same colorful hand-made pottery and the lace curtains at the window hang, sagging a little, just as they did when I left. The two-foot thick stone walls built in the 16th century give a unique quality to the light coming through the small windows. I don't know how many photographs I have taken of the dramatic light shining on one thing or another (a vase of nasturtiums, a basket of tomatoes, a geranium in a pot) sitting on that windowsill . I take a bright blue and yellow pitcher from the shelf and set it in the middle of the sill and the light just catches it as the sun descends.

As I walk up to the mezzanine, the stairs creak just a little as they always have. I have loved this place unreservedly almost as though it were a person…maybe it is the resident ghosts I adore. In any case – if it were possible to hug a house, I would hug this one! I am feeling the true comfort of being "home".

There is, however the one change in our time tested program. Usually, supper on the first night I am here is just the two of us. We have made habits over the twelve years I have been coming here for my vacation and my sanity. After twenty or so hours of traveling I'm not much good to anyone and a bite of supper and a glass of wine are all my travel-battered body needs.

Tonight it will be different.

A Parisian spinster who had no use for it had inherited another old stone house on this hilltop and close to Clare's. The spinster sold the house last year to an older Frenchman who had worked very hard making the place liveable. He has actually been living in the house for the past six-or-so months while he effected the last of the renovation.

Clare and he have become friends and while she has said little about him on the trip from Bordeaux, she smiles as she speaks of him. She has invited him for supper with us tonight – hmmm. This is a new Clare – she has not been even remotely interested in spending time with any man since Peter left – how long has it been? Maybe four - it must be five years ago!

And this man is French – Jean Bertrand is his name. I am interested to meet him but I wish my brain wasn't so jet lagged – perhaps just a little nap before supper...

No, I'd better not. If I went to sleep it would be all over until the morning.

---

* * * *

Fortunately, the rather dapper looking fellow in a laundered-and-crisply-pressed white shirt and silk cravat I met outside Clare's front door greeted me with a warm "<u>Bonsoir</u>" and quickly followed it with "Ah, and you must be <u>Margarette</u>! (He pronounces it so charmingly) I am Jean Bertrand...Jean. Clare has told me so much about you!" His dark blue eyes twinkle and he gently takes my hand and moves it to his warm lips.

I am torn between thinking:

"Thank God he speaks English!"

and

"Ohmigosh! <u>What</u> has she told him?"

But his twinkling blue eyes tell me quickly I have nothing to fear – even if she has shared secrets (and she knows some) I suspect they may be safe with him. He kisses first my left then my right cheek, takes my arm and we walk together into the house – without knocking, I note. He has done this before! I've been coming here for twelve years and I still knock.

Clare seems to become a luminous bright pink the moment we enter the kitchen. "So, Marg, you've met my new neighbor." She says, her face alight, "Jean, would you be a dear and pour us an *aperitif* while I finish this chicken?"

"Marg, sit before you fall down! We will eat soon and you can get to bed – you look like you've been run down by a truck!"

Clare sends me an indulgent smile. Count on a good friend to boost your self-image…

I glanced at the pots on the cooker. Oh, but the food smells heavenly. It seems I was hungry after all.

Jean goes first to the refrigerator where he finds a bottle of *Pineau* (a locally made combination of wine and brandy – and a favorite of mine) in the door – and then retrieves a tray of ice cubes from the freezer. By now I am wondering if he is this comfortable in his own kitchen.

He pours some of the Pineau over one ice cube in each of three tiny glasses and hands one to me and kisses the back of Clare's neck as he hands her her glass. I smile to myself. Good for her!

"Your flight was uneventful and the train predictable?" he asks me. I adore his accent – just enough to be elegant and *très* French but still easy to understand. "I hope the weather wasn't a problem in Paris. It was raining, was it not?"

"…and how would I know?" I answer. "I went from the concourse to the train station without so much as looking outside. I do love the ease with which one can get from the plane to the train without actually going into the city – of course there are worse things than <u>having</u> to go into Paris. It is one of my favorite places, for a day or two, at least. Longer than that, I'd rather be here. And I see you have arranged sunshine for me here. I thank you for that!

(Now I'm babbling.)He looks indulgent, tilting his head slightly ...forgivingly, to the side. He is a kind person.

"Jean, Clare told me you have bought old Mme. Partier's house? Are you living there all the time now?" I ask, thinking I want for him to carry the conversational ball for a while, as I cannot unmuddy my thoughts – damned jet lag!

"*Oui*, it has been...hmm...almost a year now – the house was in bad repair to begin and now at least, living here is possible while I work."

Clare interjects, "Marg, you will have to see what he has done. The place was simply a wreck - holes in the wood floor of the bedroom and also in the ceiling where water came through the broken tiles in the roof. There was no running water and no central heat – but the place is really shaping up! The fireplace in the main room is very old – the oldest part of the house, Alain tells us."

(Alain, the plumber, is a local character I have met before – and the acknowledged expert on local history.)

While I had never been inside Jean's place, I have been walking past it for years admiring the view and the fact it faces west and south – good to take advantage of the winter sunshine – and it has a cobblestoned area under an enormous and ancient walnut tree on the north side for pleasant shady suppers out of doors in the hot months. The climate here is a bit more gentle than what we are used to in Ohio, but still it is cold and damp in the winter and all these old houses and their barns are built of very local stone - much the same as my *pigeonnier*.

"How old does he think it is, Jean?" I ask.

"He says that he believes it to be 12th or 13th century, although much of the rest of the house is probably 17th. The well in the cellar is as old as the fireplace, he says, but most of the house is newer."

These Europeans have a very different frame of reference regarding what they think "newer" means... and the building methods had changed little until rather recently (that is my American assessment of "recent" -- by which I mean in the past twenty years) Now the new houses are still not built of wood, but a hollow terracotta tile. They are then covered with a sort of stucco-stuff – *crépi* - and end up looking like they might belong among the old places.

"Alain says that the old woman was born in that house as was her mother. Before that it becomes unclear, but there have been Partiers in Langnac for many generations. Alain says that Clare's house was probably also built about the same time as the original part of mine – the construction is similar in the oldest parts. Most likely it was the home of a son when he came of age to marry..."

Clare is putting the slices of *Charentais* melon, our first course, on the table at each of our places. She sits and we follow her example. Then she nods to Jean who pours each of us a glass of white wine.

"What are we drinking?" I ask.

"This is a *Cotes de Duras Blanc*, one of Clare's favorites," Jean explains. "The red for later is a Bergerac – from the vineyard of my friend Thierry. He sells no wine – he only makes enough for himself, his family and a few very lucky friends! His father and mine were in the resistance together, *le Maquis* – those two and Yves Menton's papa… Ah, they could tell some tales!"

In the midst of Jean's fascinating tale Clare replaces the melon plates with the main course. *"Bon appetit!"*

"Clare, this chicken is wonderful!" I tell her – through my jet lag I am still able to discern an elegant sauce when I taste one! This one is redolent of lemon with a bit of tarragon and lots of garlic. The chicken is fork tender and I am in heaven! She serves it simply with some of the lovely local *haricots verts,* which have been just steamed to perfection and chunks of a crusty *baguette,* with which to sop up any sauce left on the plate. Quiet descends on the little table in Clare's kitchen and we concentrate on enjoying what she has put before us.

"Clare" I tell her "you have nicely adjusted to the French way of making food and wine important priorities in life. I come back here each year because I, too, think they should be of great importance – if only to put other things in proper perspective."

Jean's eyes soften. This is a gentle, comfortable man who has moved next door to Clare – a stroke of luck for her, but then she was due for some luck.

He continues his tale as we eat our supper, "Do you know, <u>Margarette,</u> during that war the enemy lines were just here..." he gestures out the window, "...the road by Siorac at the top of that hill there. I was only a child but our fathers, Thierry, Yves and I have often said, lived several lives during those few years of war. Thierry's father was killed - we don't know by whom – and we are not certain where or precisely why. His body was found by the *forêt* just beyond that ridge of pine there. We presume a Bosch patrol caught him doing something they thought he ought not to be doing. Nothing was said. My father and Thierry's mother just buried him in the woods. It would not be safe for her if it were suspected that her husband was with the

Maquis. Better that he should simply disappear. Many did in those days."

His face in the candlelight looks younger than his sixty-some years as he recalls the days of his childhood and the very different atmosphere in this exact place, which is now the very quintessence of peace and security.

Jean continues between bites as we enjoy our supper, "It was very difficult in those days to know whom to trust. So many would sell you to the Germans for their own supposed safety – even townspeople known to you for many years. Someone in Langnac talked to the Germans. There is a monument to the tale – a stone with the names of seven men accused of being *partisans* who were shot by the Germans upon that very spot for being suspected of selling gasoline to the resistance fighters. So sad to be betrayed by your friends. My Papa, and my friends' fathers, they made their own plans and carried out their own war, trusting no one and speaking only to each other. They had, you see, been friends since they were boys and knew each others' hearts. But even within the resistance there were the true French patriots, then there were those who were with the Russian communists. And others were cowardly liars who would sell their souls to get protection from the German dogs or even from the government in *Vichy*."

I have seen in each of the small villages and hamlets in this part of France a monument at its center glorifying the "children of this place" who died in both world wars. Often, it is a four sided piece of stone with names and dates – two sides for World War I and two for World War II. Many share the same surnames. I'm sure Thierry's father's name is on the one in Langnac. A couple of years ago, I was here on VE Day and watched the ceremony in the center of town. A few musicians, both young and old, and a handful of old men proudly stuffed into their moth-bally military uniforms, stood stiffly to attention while the *Marseillaise* was played. It reminded me of our American Memorial Day ceremonies but even more somber because these men had defended their own homes, their own land – the enlisted soldiers and those who worked in this community by day and fought secretly at night as Jean's, Thierry's and Yves' fathers had.

"Jean, it is hard for me as an American to imagine what it must have been like to have the enemy just over that ridge – and literally controlling all of your life in your own homeland." I posit.

BOOM! A completely unexpected clap of thunder interrupts our reverie. I didn't hear any wind or see a flash of lightening – but to be fair – I was really into my chicken. Another! This is going to be some storm! The wind is really blowing now. Thunderstorms on this hilltop are exciting because you can see the valleys on either side and storms seem to follow the ridges. This is one of the highest around and we can see a long way. The rain begins. It pounds against the window in hard big drops. I'm glad I closed all the windows up in my little house! And I won't be walking up the hill any time soon.

"What does your friend Thierry do in Bergerac besides make very good wine?" I ask as I take another sip from my glass of red wine. Most of the "home made" wine in these parts is not made with much skill – it is a bit rough and usually pretty strong. I have tasted some and not volunteered to taste more, but this one was lovely.

"He farms. His uncle, his father's brother, Pierre, was also killed in the war and Thierry's younger brother was going to help his mother to take care of their farm here in Langnac. Thierry went to Bergerac to help his widowed aunt who had no children. The farm became his when his aunt died. His uncle was another extraordinary man. He would work all day in the orchards and on their farm and then at night he would walk, leading refugees escaping from the Germans toward the safety of the Spanish border. Often, he would walk for three hours or more, point them toward the border and safety accompanied by other of the *Maquis* and then the same distance back to his home.

They were mostly growing apricots and apples back in those days but slowly Thierry has put more of the land into vines. Now, he sells the majority of the grapes to the co-op – he only keeps the best grapes for his own. Like this wine… It is very good, *non*?"

"It is, yes! How old were you boys during the war, Jean?" I ask him.

"We were children. Ten or eleven years. Thierry, Yves, the son of the church sexton, and I grew up fast enough though. In those days everyone had a part in what was happening – even the children."

"What sort of part could a child play?" I asked.

"Well, the ease of communication we have today – cell phones and the internet – makes it hard to imagine the need, but we carried messages from hamlet to hamlet, to the resistance, you know.

"Plans were made then for one such evacuation, but in spite of all the secrecy and for whatever other reason, Thierry's father was killed and those plans abandoned…"

I found this hard to imagine, but there it was. I wondered if the child he described was he or another boy. Maybe Thierry or Yves. I tried to imagine being this child's mother or the partisan's wife - knowing your precious loved ones were taking such chances.

We finished our salads of butter lettuce, simply dressed in walnut oil and vinegar. Jean got up. He helped to clear the dishes from the table. Then, taking each bowl of ice cream as Clare scooped and then covered with a fruit *compote* fragrant with brandy with a touch of cinnamon, he brought them to the table. This aromatic topping had been warming in the oven as we ate our dinner and listened to Jean's tale.

"Would you like to go to see Thierry's vineyard, Margarette?" (I do love the way he says my name.)

"Yes, I would like to see it – whenever you want."

"I plan to go to Bergerac tomorrow late in the morning to pick up some hinges for the large *armoire* in my bedroom. You two could ride along with me and we could go to Thierry's. I really need to visit him anyway and see the vines. Perhaps we could even have lunch together. I'll call him in the morning and see if that would fit with his plans for the day."

Looking at Margaret, her ice cream now history, trying to stifle a yawn, Clare says, "Marg, it has stopped raining and it's past your bedtime, so I am throwing you out this minute. Jean and I will do these dishes and in the morning I'll come and get you for a hike. You need to get your nights and days in order."

Fact was that my eyelids had begun to close, despite Jean's gripping story. I got up. "You're right, Clare. Thanks for this lovely meal, and interesting stories. I shall see you both in the morning."

"Great. So be ready with your hiking boots on at 8:00 am sharp."

Jean interjects, "Would you please come down to my house when you return from your hike and see what Thierry has answered?"

"We will." Clare assures him.

"Now GO!" and she shooed me out the door with a smile on her face and a warm hug. "I am so glad you're here!"

I don't even remember walking up the short stone path to my little house.

Linda Conn Amstutz

Chapter FIVE

September 7, 1995 Early morning

Bellevue

The night was as though it didn't exist. I set the time on the miniature alarm clock I carry with me, so that I would be up and ready to go when Clare came to fetch me. It rang, and I got up, but my mind still felt as if it were walking through molasses in slow motion.

Like the good landlady she was, Clare had provided me with all the essentials – coffee, milk, two *croissants* and some jam. What more could a person need?

I made a pot of coffee and was lighting the oven to warm the croissants when Clare tapped on the glass of my front door. Waving her in, I set the flaky pastries in the oven and poured two cups of creamy coffee and plopped a sugar cube in mine. The little room soon began to fill with the buttery aroma of warming *croissants*.

Kissing both of Clare's cheeks and she, mine, I asked "OK, what's the scoop with this beautiful-man-neighbor of yours?"

Clare grinned but said nothing, I continued," I think he's charming, but my guess is that you think even more than that.

" How long did he stay last night? Of course, you don't have to tell me if you don't want to, but you do want to, don't you?"

"Well, it's interesting you should ask," Clare replied. "He has done such a beautiful reconstruction job on the house and asked my advice on some of the colors and such and…"

"Come on, Clare! He kissed you on the back of your neck – entirely missing both your cheeks – and men generally don't treat a decorating consultant that way - even in France! He's sweet on you." I paused. "Are you sweet on him?"

"Well, he is a really good neighbor and it is better not to be alone up here all the time…"

Now we were getting somewhere.

"When Peter left I was basically happy to be alone so that I never would feel that way again - I still am, really – but it is sort of comforting for someone to worry about you, you know? Notice if I haven't picked up the mail – or if my lights don't go on when it gets dark… I'm not getting any younger, ya know!"

Handing Clare a plate with a warm *croissant*, I told her, "Well, if you ask me – you <u>look</u> about ten years younger than the last time I saw you." She hadn't been exactly depressed – by a clinical definition – but she hadn't written anything since Peter left, and it's a good thing her books were still selling or she might have had a serious lack of cash.

Last September, I heard her on the phone with her publisher, and she didn't make excuses, exactly – she said she simply "had nothing to write". Her mysteries, which were set just a few years in the future, used to be all the rage, first in England and then after that in the States. Clare even had two titles at once for a short while on the New York Times Best Seller List!

Now she takes care of her garden, sings in the church choir and has lunch with friends from time to time, but there has been no one even trying to take Peter's place in her life – if they had tried, she'd have turned them to stone with one of her "looks". Nope, Clare wasn't interested in opening herself up for more of what Peter left her with – it was at the very least "nothing to write".

"Well, if he is worried about you, that seems a good beginning. Finish your coffee and let's get going before I nod off again. Then you can tell me what you foresee for the middle and the ending…"

I got up and walked out the door and took hold of my walking stick – which was still leaning on the wall next to the doorway precisely where I left it last September – I do love this place!

"C'mon, Clare! I bought myself a pedometer so we won't have to guess how far we walk – we will know down to the last tenth of a mile...er...kilometre!

We walked first eastward, so that at the end of our circuit we would walk past Jean's house where we would stop and see just what time we should be ready to leave to visit his friend's vineyard in Bergerac.

The unpaved lane through the woods took us across to the "ridge road" and then back through a farm at the bottom of the hill. Then we walked through another woods and up to the west end of the road upon which we started. About an hour's circuit – some uphill and some down – nothing too steep... A good beginning to the day and a pleasant experience whether done alone or in the company of a friend.

This morning was particularly beautiful; the rain of last night had washed the air and the sky was a bright clear (French?) blue. The birds sang and everything smelled of...what is this smell? Lichen? Mushrooms? Wet wood? Decomposing leaves? Damp earth? A heavenly and earthly mixture. It would be hot later in the day but just now it was perfect for getting our exercise out of the way and making a productive start to the day.

"Oh, did I tell you I am working on a new book?" Clare asked casually as if it had been a month she finished the last one.

"No, you didn't. Is it another of the "Lefty" stories?"

"Actually, it isn't. I have a new character who is a bit soft compared to Lefty, the hard-bitten police chief. She…"

"SHE?" I gasped. "Your new character is a woman? Holy cow! Can you <u>do</u> that?"

"I'm trying! I'll let you see a bit of what I have written and you can tell me what you think."

Clare's novels have few if any female characters – she has always said men were so much simpler and she felt she could make them believable. Women were so "complicated". This is a real departure for my buddy who seems to be departing in all directions these days. I knew better than to ask her any more, she'd already told me more than she usually did before the first draft was ready for an editor.

Peter, whose departure put an end to the Lefty series, at least for the short term, was a "one of a kind" person. There are those who would say that was a good thing. Personally, I really liked him. He was a good friend to me and I have no sad stories like Clare has. She had literally followed him to the ends of the earth and she thought he was as invested in their partnership as she was. They sailed in the eastern Mediterranean for several years then lived along the beautiful coast in Yugoslavia for a few more and finally found this place and most of the renovation done to this farmhouse was done while he was still here. He could be very handy and a hard worker. From time to time he would leave for a few weeks and go sailing with friends or ride his bicycle in a French race but then he came "home". He tried to stay here but the wanderlust in his soul got the better of him and Clare felt she had wandered enough – so the decision was made. He left and she stayed.

A year or so later it was a clear autumn morning much like this one - and he was cycling along above the Rhone River and a truck full of *Provençal* melons destined for Parisian tables rumbled past on the narrow road and just barely nudged his bicycle – but there was no space for him to recover his balance and the sweet man who had been my friend and Clare's partner went off the edge and down nearly 300 meters before coming to rest in a small tributary of the mighty Rhone. There are no more adventures on this earth for Peter, and I am missing a dear friend and there will be no reconciliation for him and Clare. He left Clare for the last time five years ago. She has been different since then. She hasn't had the old sparkle and she hasn't written …until now. I don't think Clare exactly "needs" a man to be productive in her writing, I think it is more that she was simply so desperately unhappy when Peter left that her creative spirit was put to sleep - or something like that - maybe she just woke up?

We just came around the edge of the woods and the valley opened up before us – there simply aren't words to adequately describe this view. Generations of French farmers put their sweat and toil into making the patchwork of sunflowers, wheat and cornfields, the odd vineyard and some pasture. A wisp of ground fog lay in the bottom near a pond and the neighbor's cows, pale tan and sorrel-colored, were already lying down for their morning nap.

"Damned jet lag," I murmured, as much to myself as to Clare. "I forgot to put my camera in my pocket! Well, we will just stand here for a moment and burn this image into our memories."

We fall into companionable silence as we enjoy the idyllic scene in front of us.

Clare lives here full time and she still is just as awed by the beauty of it as I am. The walnut trees form a line at the top of the ridge, and the brilliant sea of yellow of the field is, of course, sunflowers, grown for their healthy oil more than for their smiling faces.

A small orchard of apple and pear trees lies just to the left and then, of course there are the grapes – grown around here only in small, well-tended plots for personal use by the farmer. East of here, nearer to Bergerac and Bordeaux, where the soil gets more gravelly and the hills face to the east and south, are the real vineyards - large but equally well-tended. They go on as far as the eye can see; rolling in precise rows over hills and the evidence of individual attention to each vine makes the sight fascinating to a "wino" like me. I am truly looking forward to our trip to Bergerac!

We continued our walk through the woods and up along the lane to a stone fence in front of Jean's house. He has painted his shutters a shade of purplish blue I would describe as "heliotrope", I think, and I like the effect - the pale buff color of the limestone and the blue of the shutters. He hasn't planted any flowers but he has trimmed the fig tree and the old roses and the grapevine which grows over the door. You can tell the place is inhabited, now.

The door is slightly ajar – he must have anticipated our arrival – Clare smiled as she sang out "Jean! Bonjour! "We're here!" as she casually pushed the door open to allow our entry. "Jean? Where are you?"

The front door opens directly into the large kitchen – well, it is the main sitting room also, typical of a French farmhouse

On the table are a "bowl" of café au lait and half of a piece of toasted *baguette,* a crumpled red printed cotton napkin beside the plate.

Clare called out again, "Jean! We stopped to see what time you wanted to go to Bergerac. Jean?"

There was no sound – save the twittering of the birds outside. I thought perhaps we'd hear the telltale sound of the plumbing and then he would appear…

So, while Clare went further through the house in search of Jean, I took a good look around. He had clearly made some major changes.

The kitchen was large and light as a result of the new front door made of eight square panes of glass and the double French doors on the far side – a fairly recent construction and a great improvement over the original dark solid rock wall! I peeked through the French doors which opened to the cobbled terrace. A round stone table stood out there and some teak chairs for al fresco dining in good weather.

The floor was made up of ancient lozenge-shaped terracotta tiles, polished and gleaming. The ceiling was open to the rafters of natural wood – old and some of them as twisted as the trees from which they had been cut. At the end of the room the ancient fireplace resided. A couple of comfortable chairs covered in soft looking deep tan leather nestled close to an elegant cylindrical deep blue enameled wood-burning stove with a glass door through which one could see a cheerful fire on chilly nights in the winter. There was also evidence of central heating along the north facing walls so that when it was really cold, the house would be cozy and warm.

An ancient stone sink – in the house from its beginning, I suspected, sat between some simple tall dark wooden cupboards, much-mellowed by polish and sunken into the walls. The appliances in the kitchen area were new and of the best quality. Copper and enamel pots hung from a brass rack over an island built to house the stove – proof that either he cooked or he was expecting "someone" would do some significant culinary creating with the shiny deep-red gas-fired *La Cornue* cooker.

I'm jealous; I have hankered after a *La Cornue* cooker since I learned of their existence. (He is French after all

– probably HE cooks.) The walls were white or the natural stone and devoid of decoration – all the color in the room came from the various traditionally bright *Provençal* prints of the curtains, tablecloth, and cushions on the chairs and the comfy overstuffed couch. It was a room to live in happily– Clare was right - he has done a remarkable job!

He has also put a chunk of money into this project, even considering he has done much of the labor himself. The appliances were costly, as were the fabrics he has used. The old floor tiles were not typical of this area and they had to be found and transported and then laid – a job for a specialist – I think M. Bertrand must have some significant resources...as I thought that I remembered last night, several times I thought to ask him what the had done before he retired and I got sidetracked listening to his entrancing stories. Jet lag.

"Jean? Where are you?" Clare called again. By now, she sounded really worried.

We had been here for maybe five minutes and he had not answered.

"Wait a moment," Clare said and went outside. "I'll see if his car's in the barn."

"No problem. I'll stay here in case he turns up."

When she reentered the room she said, "Marg, something isn't right here. He was expecting for us to come by. His coffee is still warm and his car is in the barn – where could he be?"

Now, I, too was getting concerned. Together, we looked in the bedroom, bathroom, and even lifted the trap door to look down in the cellar – he was nowhere to be found.

"I think we would have heard a car in the lane, don't you? He can't have been gone that long…and the front door was open. This isn't right!" Clare was slowly getting worked up. "I saw him at 7:30 this morning and he was fine. If he was ill and called someone because we were gone on our hike he'd at least have locked the door when he left…if he could… Oh, Marg!" Clare threw her hands to her cheeks and I could see the tears forming in her eyes. "I'm afraid something has happened to him. What should we do?"

"You're asking me? You'd have a better idea than I would. If I were at home I'd call the hospitals – oh, there is a hospital in Langnac, isn't there? And maybe the police – *gendarmes*? Let's close his door and go back to your house and make some phone calls." I hesitated. "Wait, let's leave a note to say that he should call us in case he comes back here. Does he have a cell phone?"

"Oh, yes! Why didn't I think of that? I'll use this phone and call his cell..." She pushed the keys of the telephone on the counter and the very worst thing happened.

Linda Conn Amstutz

Chapter SIX

September 7, 1995 Mid-Morning

Bellevue

The first few notes of Beethoven's Fifth Symphony rang out from under his napkin on the table next to his cooling bowl of coffee.

Wherever Jean had gone he hadn't taken his cell phone with him. Now I was getting goose bumps.

It hit Clare the same way. She looked at me as she replaced the receiver on the house phone and the notes of the ring-tone ceased as now real tears formed in her eyes.

"I can't lose him," she said,. "I just can't. Oh Marg!"

I walked over and put my arm around her shoulder, trying to sound more optimistic than I felt. "There is a logical explanation for this. We just have to figure out what it is."

I spoke with, I hoped, the sound of confidence, though I had none.

The balance of the morning went like this:

We returned the short distance to Clare's house but the phone calls Clare made to the *gendarmes* and hospital yielded nothing.

When she called Thierry's home in Bergerac to see if perhaps Jean had gone there.(without his car?) She got no answer in spite of the fact she tried three times.

Eventually, we busied ourselves making a salad lunch in Clare's kitchen to distract ourselves. When all else fails…eat!

Clare and I looked at each other feeling stupid and helpless. We sat at the table and began to pick at our food. There was almost no conversation – anything we could say sounded even scarier than we felt already. What could have happened?

Then we both started talking at once.

"It's OK; he'll come back soon," said Clare at the same time I was saying, "Let's not worry. He'll be along any time." And we both laughed nervously and knew neither of us believed what the other was saying.

We ate our lunch - a salad made with *frisée* lettuce – a nice bitter green in contrast to the richness of the warm breadcrumb-crusted patty of fresh goat cheese and the perfectly ripe slice of tomato. Afterwards, Clare made us each a cup of tea from the lemon verbena in her garden and sat down again.

"Marg, I didn't even know I was lonely. I was so hurt after Peter left, I was just glad to be alone so that no one could ever do that to me again. For years, that was comfortable and all I wanted. Then Jean showed up."

She sighed.

"Neighbors out here in the country are important. We are isolated here, especially in the winter months, and it is good to know who is living close to you should you need some help. Well, the first day I saw a car in the lane beside old Mme. Partier's place I walked up the drive. There was a large broken limb from the oak tree across it so a car couldn't pass. I hollered in the front door, 'hello' – and this adorable man came up from the cellar, his head festooned in cobwebs and smiling that lovely warm smile of his...

Clare, eyes brimming with tears, took a deep breath and continued.

"He grew up in here in Langnac, you see, and after his schooling he went to work in Paris. He's an architect, specializing in the restoration of public buildings." Clare smiled as she explained, she liked talking about him - it made her feel closer, I thought.

"He loved working in the city and was, I think, quite successful, but when he retired – about a year and a half ago - he began looking for a house near to Langnac. Jean loves this town and still has many friends here. His family home was in the centre and when his parents were both gone, he had it sold because he knew that when he came back he would want a place away – not far away, but in the countryside. I am just lucky he came upon this one! Old Mme. Partier's daughter lives in Paris now and didn't want to be bothered with the house, and it was such a wreck that no one else wanted it – thank God!

I told her "He was lucky to find a place with such a good neighbor."

67

"That first night I offered supper, if he promised to leave the cobwebs at his house." She smiled."In fact, he came here for a shower as his water was not connected yet. He is so pleasant to be with, never moody, and he is so talented! You saw what he has done with that house. He really enjoys to work with his hands. Most of his career he had to leave that sort of work for others to do, when he really just wanted to get his hands dirty and get in touch with the old places he was restoring…

"Jean knows so much about the history of this place and how the old farmhouses were built – I have learned loads from him. The well in my cellar and the fireplace in the back room go back to the origins of his house! But he told you that, didn't he?"

I nodded. "Yes, he did." Memories of last night flooded back. Theirs had been a thorough conversation, like amongst old friends.

"Well, you know, it is just as easy to cook for two as it is for one, maybe easier, so we began to eat our evening meal together – when he was here working on the house. And then when he wasn't here I began to feel as if one of my limbs were missing. I started writing to get my mind off his absence, I think – it has been very good for me.

"Jean is such good company. I thought he was just grateful to have a hot meal after working hard all day but it has become more – for both of us. Did he tell you he was married once, long ago? She left him for an older and richer man. Since then, he felt much the same as I have. It is best to be alone – to protect your feelings – but we have grown to trust each other…and more. Oh, Marg – what has happened to him?"

"If only he had left a message…" she mused wishfully.

I had a thought "Why don't you call Roberta?" (Roberta Cartier is Clare's other neighbor on this hilltop and one likely to know someone else's business!)

"If anyone saw or heard something this morning, Roberta's the lady who did!" I said. "I'll bet she knows something! Better yet – let's go over there and talk with her. I'd like to see her."

So we were off to the Cartier's.

Roberta and Conrad are an interesting pair – she is English and he is Belgian. They met each other and married in Singapore where they both worked when they were young. They retired here about five years ago – just about the time Peter left – and while Conrad is happy to putter forever in his garden, Roberta needs to be involved with what goes on in this community – at least the English speaking part of it.

Their house is newer than the others up on this hilltop – one of those built with the hollow terracotta tiles covered with stucco. It is a very pleasant place, with a tower (from which you can watch the sun set), a swimming pool and a capacious and thriving garden nurtured by Conrad. He spent his working years as an accountant for a large multinational company. His job kept him indoors most of the time. He did his job well and precisely but repressed his need to grow things in the soil – until his retirement. Now he is…overcompensating - in my opinion, of course.

Actually, I think it may be Roberta's opinion also, though I have not heard her voice it. She is the one who is expected to make use of the prodigious production from his efforts. For example, last summer I remember her waxing eloquent about the bountiful harvest of tomatoes brought basketful after basketful to her by a proud Conrad – which she canned and canned and canned and then quietly provided to neighbors and friends, and in the end any strangers who didn't think of a polite way to refuse quickly enough or didn't lock their car doors in her driveway. And then there were the beans and zucchini and the artichokes and don't mention the word "fig" to Roberta…

But Conrad is a happy man now, digging and planting and weeding and harvesting.

Roberta has learned her preserving skills late in life – she spent her working days and years as a secretary for the British Foreign Service – there was always a place for her in whatever city Conrad was assigned to work in and she loved being "in on the action" in each posting. She is fun to be around and has her finger on the pulse of this place, just as she did in all the others.

I realised just how much I had missed Roberta as soon as she opened the front door! She grabbed me in a strong bear hug and verbalised just what I had been thinking - "Marg! When did you arrive, God how I have missed you!"

She is attractive and fiery henna-haired though she could benefit by adding a pound or two – she seems never to be at rest – always tuned into what is going on around her - which is why we walked the hundred meters or so up the lane to ask "Have you seen anything of Clare's neighbour Jean?"

"Not a thing, ladies, sorry. I'm afraid I wasn't as ambitious as the two of you – I stayed up too late last night painting [a hobby recently acquired] and slept in until after nine this morning. I seldom do that, but this morning I did. Why don't you ask Conrad? He may have been in the garden. He's just on the terrace. Can I offer you some tea, or something cold to drink?"

"Tea would be lovely, thanks," I said and Claire agreed as we went out to their verandah overlooking the pool and beyond, in the distance, the valley and the main road into Langnac.

"Conrad! You're looking well, my friend!" I began. "Have you been in the garden all morning (though I suspected the answer from looking at the mud on his boots by the door)?"

"Why, yes, I have, Marg. It is good to see you! Are you here for a long visit this year or a short one?" he asked, rising from his chair and kissing both my cheeks.

"A month, Conrad. It looks long enough today, as I just arrived, but when it is time to go, I'm afraid, like always, it will seem to be way too short. Got here last evening but parts of my brain are, I think, still traveling. I hope they catch up soon."

He laughed. "Oh, I'm sure they will. Make yourselves comfortable, ladies."

He sat down again and we settled into the comfortable garden chairs.

"Conrad, we were supposed to meet our new neighbor, Jean Bertrand, this morning for a trip into Bergerac, but he seems to be gone," I said. "His door was open, and Clare and I are puzzled as to why he would go so abruptly as to leave the door open. Did you happen to see him this morning?"

Conrad thought for a moment, rubbing his as yet unshaved chin. "Just before Roberta rose I saw a car on the *chemin rural* [the lane between the Cartiers' and Clare's] but I didn't recognize it. A small white van – like the truck of the *boulangerie,* and it was going very fast. At least for that pot-holed lane, it was! Are you concerned for him? It does seem odd for him to have left the door open."

"Yes, we are concerned. This van must have come just before we got back from our hike. We sure didn't see it or hear it."

"Which way did it go?" Clare asked.

"Down the hill to the main road, I think. Not past here, certainly. I would have noticed that... The only reason I remember it at all was because I thought at first it might be the post but he doesn't drive that fast. And it seemed awfully early for that. He is not usually here until nearly eleven. Then I saw it was a white van and not the little yellow post car. Sorry, I can't be more help."

Roberta had arrived with the tea in the middle of this not very fruitful conversation and we settled in for what she called a "natter". We caught up on what was going on with her children and what travel she and Conrad had planned for the near future and sipped our tea. It seemed very civilized – and all the while I was having visions of kidnappers or brigands or worse! Oh, my!

When Clare and I left and walked back to Bellevue I wished my mind was clearer – and that I had some idea of what could have happened to Jean. And I wanted something palliative I could offer to my friend who was silently so worried about this man who had become very important to her.

As we approached her house, Clare suddenly snapped her fingers. "Yves! I'll call Yves and see if perhaps he knows what is going on with Jean – if Thierry isn't around to answer the phone. Yves is the third part of their 'triumvirate'!"

"That's a great idea! Do you have the number or do we have to go down to Jean's and try to find it?" I asked, quickening my pace to match hers.

"No, I have it!"

We practically ran to her house and straight to the telephone.

This day was destined to be fraught with frustration – and telephone answering machines. Yves' phone rang and rang, then his answering machine took Clare's plaintive message asking him to call her back if he had any idea where Jean had got to.

"Please help!" she added at the end, then hung up.

I walk over to her and pull her into a brief embrace.

"Clare, I'm going to lay my poor tired head down and see if it works any better when it has had some time on the pillow. Maybe we meet in the yard for an aperitif – say about seven?"

"OK, I'll bring us something to munch on and you bring the wine. I left several bottles on the shelf just above the refrigerator and there also is some Pineau in your fridge if you'd prefer that. I don't care one way or the other."

My heart hurt for her – this poor, lonely woman who had not thought anyone's absence could make her feel this bad again…

Linda Conn Amstutz

Chapter SEVEN

September 7, 1995 – late afternoon

Bellevue

There was no sleep for me. I squeezed my eyes shut and they popped open again. The brain was still foggy, but after coffee for breakfast and then tea after lunch the caffeine was working! I lay in my narrow bed upstairs and thought of what we knew about Jean's disappearance and what we needed to find out. There was an issue nagging my thoughts but just slightly out of reach...

There was something Jean was telling us last night that he didn't actually say but I heard all the same. I have spent the past thirty years as a salesman (OK, "salesperson" – but I always maintained if I could do the job they could call me a salesman, no harm, no foul) and the primary valuable attribute a salesman can have is not, as many believe, the "gift of gab" but rather the ability to listen – to truly hear – both what the person speaking says but also beyond that to what the person really wants you to know. It seemed last night that there was something that Jean was not saying that he wanted me to know. And it is in my brain somewhere if only I knew where to look.

I sat on the edge of the bed and looked out at the panorama of farm fields and old stone houses punctuated by the occasional walnut tree. I saw the hedgerows and the placid tan-colored cows that can put peace in your soul simply by looking at them and whose ancestors had traced the indirect paths followed now by the country roads. I tried to imagine what sort of aberrant mind it would take to make a battlefield of the place I was now looking at. How could you fool with the bucolic perfection of this scene? And further, how would it feel to have an enemy violate your home – your farm, your land, your town, your family!? To what lengths would I go to rid my place on this earth of such a demon? The French describe this time as one of "*un sentiment du viol*" – or, as we would say, "rape."

I tried to think as a parent of one of those boys who rode their bicycles the short distance from here to school in Langnac or to their friend's farm in Siorac (which was across the German lines). How could you allow your child to be exposed to such danger? What would go through your mind as you watched him turn out of the safety of your own courtyard and pedal up the road into who knows what? And why? Wouldn't I rather have my son alive than fight some political battle? Or is liberty so deeply ingrained in the French soul (or my American one for that matter) that it would be worth your life or the life of your child or your husband to do a small part to preserve it – or regain it?

And what part was played by the women in this resistance effort? Last night, Jean had spoken of the fathers and the boys but the only thing he said about the women was that Thierry's mother had helped Jean's father bury her husband in the woods. And where was that?

He had gestured toward that woods to the east, I think…Oh, God, to have a hand in digging the hole and physically pushing the still warm body of your beloved husband and the father of your children into it; to gaze one last time at his dear face and then to shovel dirt on it; to look forward to the aching loneliness of widowhood made even worse by the privation of war. And then to see your son take on the role of his father in everything: the farm work, your security and even the venture into the very danger that had got his father killed. This woman must have been made of very stern stuff. I wondered if she were still living.

I could compensate somewhat for the fuzz in my head with a pencil and paper list…so I found a tablet in the top drawer of the nightstand (just where I left it) and the stub of a pencil and began. I listed what I knew about Jean and his friends – both back in the days of their childhood and in the present. I found that Jean had actually told me more about back then than he had about now. Then I thought about the questions I had – both last night and this morning.

– Which boy had been the one who had carried the message?

- What was the message and why was it so vital?

- How was it related to Thierry's father's death, or was that a separate story?

- Was the message about something with which we are still concerned?

That was the underlying thing I was getting from Jean last night! That was what he hadn't said that we were supposed to hear! I am almost sure of it. He had said he "really needed to see Thierry."

I thought if I could talk with Yves there might be something he would be able to clarify; somehow he could help.

Before I finished writing that thought on my list I was up and out the door. I quickly made my way into the barn and unwrapped my bicycle from the plastic sheet in which I had wrapped it last fall to preserve it from the barn dust and bird droppings. I took the pump off its nail on the wall and added a bit of air to both the tires to make up for what had escaped during its eleven month rest and hopped on.

I rode out – leaving the barn door open as a signal to Clare I'd gone for a bike ride (and so she shouldn't worry – she had enough on her mind) – and headed into Langnac. What I knew about Yves was that he was, like both his father and grandfather before him, the sexton of the church – the *sacristain* – so I would begin looking there. If he didn't answer his phone earlier, it must be that he was at the church and I knew just where that was.

The ride into town was, except for a few very short sections, nearly all downhill – gently descending out here in the country but, once you get into Langnac, precipitously steep. The good news is that the old church is at the top of the precipitous part. My bicycle's brakes worked just fine but they made an awful racket, and I wouldn't have to alert the whole town of my arrival with them if I stopped at the church!

The *sacristain's* little house is just behind the apse end of the church that was built, along with many others in this region of France, in the 11th century. It was a (rare) time of peace, of population growth and of the expansion of a network of Christian parishes. When the Langnac Église de Notre Dame was built, and shortly thereafter during the Hundred Years' War, it was used not only as a place of worship but also as a fortress. The simple semicircular arches identify Romanesque churches, and while some have pointy gothic touches added later, this one is nearly pure Romanesque in its style.

Between the road and the simple stone house was a large and well-tended garden. So, now I knew something else about Yves – he was a gardener and a good one! Both vegetables and flowers grew and flourished in this patch and there was another area near to the door, raised and surrounded with cut limestone where several types of herbs grew: thyme, parsley, sage, sorrel, oregano and a couple I didn't recognize. Just next to the door was a bush of bay laurel. A cook, either Yves or his wife – though I didn't know whether he had a wife - lived here. I passed by the house, leaned my bicycle into the fence surrounding the churchyard and walked to the steps leading up to the large carved doorway in the front. After a moment's hesitation, I lifted the latch and let myself in.

No sooner had I closed the door behind me than the organ began to play, as if it were automated to come on as the door was opened! I jumped and took a startled breath. But there was no phantom of Langnac Notre Dame – an older man was sitting at the console working the stops and running his fingers over the keyboard. Actually, the organ was apparently a rather new one and looked quite large for this small and unassuming country church, but the sound was good and the player seemed to have some skill.

I sat in the last pew and listened for a while, hoping Yves, or someone looking like a caretaker, would show up. Surely the caretaker, the sexton, the *sacristain*, doesn't also play the organ! But this is a small town, and I was possibly making a wrong assumption.

When he stopped to find another piece of printed music I walked up and asked him, *"Où est la sacristain, s'il vous plaît?"* (Where is the sexton, please?)

He answered in English, "It is *le sacristain* not *la sacristain*, and he is just here before you!" And he gave me a big and friendly smile.

"Are you Yves?" I asked.

"And who would like to have this information, if I might be so bold as to inquire?"

"I'm sorry, my name is Margaret O'Connor. I am a friend of Clare Williams, who is the neighbor of Jean Bertrand – who, I understand, is a friend of yours. Am I right?" I babbled.

A step in the right direction – at least I had found him.

He was as attractive as his friend and about the same age – but ruddy and wavy-haired where Jean's was straight. His brown eyes – well, sort of a soft caramel color and very direct – looked into my soul as we spoke. He was taller than most Frenchmen and lanky like an adolescent. His hair was longish, a sandy reddish-brown color flecked with gray, now, and caught in a retro-hippie ponytail at the nape of his neck. When he smiled his whole face beamed – none of this mouth-turned-up-at-the-corners stuff for him. Even his ears moved with the force of his smile! A battered beret of a fairly indeterminate hue peeked out from his back pocket (I guess because he was inside the church), and he wore a sort of tunic of soft navy blue canvas over his blue jeans. I wasn't sure if it were some sort of uniform for sextons or just his idea of style. In either case, it was fine with me - he looked delicious!

I hadn't met Thierry yet – but these three must have been quite the lady-killers in their day. Of course that day hadn't entirely passed, given my reaction to the two of the three of them I have met – but they are "mature and good looking" now, not the drop dead gorgeous young men they must have been thirty years ago.

"I am happy to meet you, Mme. O'Connor. Are you staying with Clare while you are here in Langnac?" he asked.

"Yes, I am living in her *pigeonnier* for the next four weeks. Clare and I are longtime friends – almost as long a time as you and Jean. Please call me Margaret."

He smiled at me again. "*Enchanté*, Margaret. Is there something I can do for you?"

"Yves, I am - we are – concerned for Jean's welfare. He was planning to meet with us this morning and we were going to drive to Bergerac to run an errand for him and then meet your friend Thierry, and he seems to have just disappeared - Jean, I mean. He left his door open and his cell phone behind and a still warm cup of coffee stood on the table, untouched. His car is also still there but he is just...gone!" I paused to catch my breath, then continued. "Jean hasn't been home all day, and he has not contacted Clare to say why he aborted our plans. She is really concerned and so am I. Have you any idea where he might have gone?"

The smile vanished, and a couple of lines appeared between his eyebrows. His whole visage changed.

Eventually, he said, "I think you should not worry about Jean,; he will be just fine. You should tell Clare the same. Believe me, he can take care of himself. He will be alright."

I didn't believe him. Taking a breath, I decided to find another approach as he seemed to have thought he put the subject to rest (and distract me?), so I agreed when Yves suggested, "Why don't you let me show you around our very ancient church? This organ is new, a gift from a parishioner who also likes to play it. I, of course was pleased when he presented it to us as I enjoy playing as well. I am not good at it, of course, but I find music a pleasant pastime, and the acoustics here are very nice."

He knew something. I couldn't rid myself of the sensation. He seemed sincerely certain no harm has come to Jean but he was not sharing whatever it is that he knew either. I don't like having a smokescreen put up like this. When I asked him a direct question I wanted a direct answer. But then, he doesn't know me from Adam, and if the reason is a sensitive one, of course he wouldn't tell me everything. So, I should get to know him better and see if perhaps then he would help us to find his friend. I would take his guided tour of the church and "make-nice" with him.

He showed me the seventeenth century fresco in the cupola and the gothic windows, the semicircular arches built with local limestone and the dropped keystones. But he <u>didn't</u> volunteer to show me the fortifications which must have been in this church from the very earliest construction…which I thought was just a bit odd. That feature should have been "on the tour". But it is a wonderful old church and, unlike many of its contemporaries, very little changed from the beginning – a few windows, and that is about all that has been altered. He is a delightful man when he was not trying to pull the proverbial wool over my eyes, and I liked him in spite of that.

I left after suggesting that he come to visit us at Bellevue.

I went straight home to my *pigeonnier*, but rather than go directly to Clare and tell her all I didn't know, I decided to think about it a little. I also wanted to add some details to my penciled list and see if I could make some sense of it. Sometimes it is better to ruminate on things rather than spit them right out – especially since Clare seems to be so sort of "raw" about this whole thing…

Yves was definitely hiding something.

Linda Conn Amstutz

Chapter EIGHT

September 7, 1995 the hour of the aperitif

Bellevue

My plan was to tell Clare what I had learned, over a restorative glass of crisp white wine, and then to ask her some questions also.

It didn't work out quite that way.

I was carrying two glasses in one hand and an open bottle of chilled white Bordeaux in the other as I made my way to the little stone table halfway between Clare's house and my *pigeonnier*. From that spot there is a lovely view of our valley, and it is a purely elegant place on a summer evening for a restorative *aperitif*…

"Marg!" Clare must have spotted me from the window. "Where have you been? I saw the barn door open and figured you'd ridden your bike somewhere but I had no idea where. Your office called. They wanted to talk with you, and I didn't know what to tell them." She paused when she reached me. "They said you should call them the very minute you returned!"

Oops, I guess I should have told her I was back…

I sighed. No *aperitif* for me, not this evening, not at this moment anyhow.

I poured the pale straw-colored wine in each of the glasses and handed one to Clare. She sat gazing over the valley and I headed for the house taking the other one with me into Clare's kitchen. "I'll be back as soon as I can!" I said, with all the optimism I could muster.

I dialed the seemingly endless string of numbers necessary to connect with my office and have my credit card charged for the very expensive call, rather than to put the charge on Clare's phone bill.

Harry answered.

"What are you doing answering the phone?" I asked him. "Where's Lila? And what is going on?"

Harry replied, "I am answering the phone because everyone but me has gone to lunch. I was waiting for you to call back so I can tell you about the Hardy account. We got it! We got the contract for the next year!"

"But I thought they were not going to make the decision until next month when I'm back."

"Yes, but old Mr. Hardy got tired of young Jeff's dithering around and he had some radio spots he needed to place now – this month - to get the pre-holiday discount. He couldn't do it without solidifying the plans for next year so... we got it!"

"That's great news, Harry. Thanks for letting me know."

"Wait! The trouble is... I can't sign it. You have to do it. So I FedExed it to you. You should have it by noon tomorrow and you could then overnight it back to me. Aren't you pumped? This is such a good feeling! It really gives us all a good foundation to build on for the next 12 months. It means at the very least over $200,000 in revenues! Probably more like $400,000 by the time they add the catalog CD and... Oh, well – you knew that..."

Now, about this time I was really feeling torn. I was certainly pleased about the solidification of The Hardy Group's business, but I was also a little miffed that it hadn't been me who persuaded old Mr. Hardy to accelerate the process. I wanted Harry to succeed – it would help me to get paid…but I guess I was just a little jealous.

Instead, what I told Harry was, "You are a proper genius, Harry, and I think there is possibly be a future for you in this field. I will get the contract right back to you. What else is new at the office?"

He hesitated a moment. "Not much. Oh! Lila's pregnant. She says she can't afford to take much time with no salary, and if we let her bring the baby in with her she won't take any time off at all. What do you think?"

"I think that will be your decision as it won't take place until you're the one in charge! And I won't have to worry about it. How do you like them apples, Mr. Lane?"

"OK, good…" he replied, pausing to reflect for a moment upon his new responsibilities. "This phone call is pretty expensive, Marg – we'd better cut it short. I really just wanted to warn you that the Hardy papers were coming for you to sign and to tell you things seem to be going smoothly. You shouldn't worry about us. Bye for now…"

"Byc, Harry...and thanks. You did a good job with the Hardys."

Now, I am an adult. I shouldn't allow a little thing like that bother me. I should be just purely happy that the office seems to be running smoothly in my absence and that Harry will be able to handle the helm of my little agency with grace and style when he becomes the owner. And I am happy and proud of him – I do think he will do fine while I am gone. But there is that irksome little voice that nags me and says, "How will you get along when you don't have this to do any longer, and someone else is getting the satisfaction you have enjoyed for twenty years?" ...and I don't know how...I just don't know.

A swallow of wine, and I was ready to go outside and shift gears once again into the problem of what has become of Jean Bertrand.

As I approached her, Clare was gazing over the sunflower field and I could almost hear what she is thinking "Jean, where are you? Why didn't you let us know where you were going? Are you all right? Are you hurt? Where are you?"

What she actually said when I got there was, "What was that all about? Is everything OK at home?"

"Yeah, fine. Actually it was good news – our biggest client has renewed their contract early! So there is hope that this deal will work out for all of us… Harry sent the contract overnight for me to sign. It should be here sometime tomorrow morning."

"Ah, I hope they'll find us out here." She smiled.

I settled into a vacant chair, taking in the beautiful scenery.

Shifting gears, I finally said to Clare, "Earlier, I went into Langnac and stopped by the church where I met Yves. He was sure nothing bad has happened to Jean, but he acted almost like he knew where Jean was, although he didn't actually verbalise that. He just said that I should tell you not to worry and that Jean will be fine. Then he insisted upon giving me a tour of the church." I paused, sorting the questions in my head "Wasn't this church used as place for the people to hide in the Hundred Years' War? Most of these Romanesque churches were. I remember reading that somewhere. Was this one different?"

"No, it's not. It is fortified, though. The whole dome is actually two layers with a space in the middle where both the townspeople and the *seigneur's* (landlord's) family barricaded themselves for safety. Didn't he show you the entry? That is usually the highlight of the tour – his favorite part to explain about."

"Nope, he didn't, but he played the organ for me. Or, actually, he was playing the organ as I slipped in and I listened to him until he stopped. He is quite good, but it is a big organ for such a small church."

"I didn't know they had finished putting it in! They have been working on installing the pipes for months - nearly a year! That is great. You see, the organ was a gift to the church from the owner of the chateau on the other side of the main road – above the river." Clare waved a hand vaguely in that direction. "He could have installed that organ in the great hall of the chateau but instead gave it to the church and he can now play it there, and the church can use it too. They, that is, Yves, will care for it and he is also permitted to play it. It has been a difficult installation because the church is so old and there were complications because it is some sort of historical landmark, or some such thing, Jean was trying to explain it to me and I wasn't paying much attention. Anyhow, I am happy to know that it is all done. So…exactly what did Yves say about Jean?"

"That was it! He said to tell you Jean would be fine," I repeated.

"Then we don't know any more than we did before?" Clare asked.

"Well, maybe we do. I think Yves knows more than he is letting on – a lot more; like he knows where Jean is and what he is doing and he is not, definitely not, telling us. That is what I think." I said emphatically.

"Why?" asked Clare.

"Why do I think that? Or why isn't he telling us what he knows?"

She shrugged.

"I think that because, well, call it intuition, a feeling, a look in his eye…whatever. I have no idea why he isn't telling us what he knows unless he thinks that for us to know might jeopardize Jean's safety. That is pure- ly a guess. How well do you know Yves? Maybe he is being this way because he just doesn't know me at all," I rambled.

"You could be right. There is a bond among those three that is strong and very special and, though I have only seen them together, all three, a couple of times, I am sure they can be counted on to protect each other against any threat. This friendship goes far into their history and spans many years and many sorts of shared experiences which most people only read about." She gave me a sideways glance. "Did you like him? I do. I like all three of them. They are moral and ethical and bright and a lot of fun to be around, not to mention a pleasure to look at – even at my age," Clare gushed.

I laughed. "Whew! So what do we do now?" I asked, sobering.

Clare's answer was to pour two more glasses of wine and put her feet up on the little stone table and gaze into the distance.

"I don't know."

Linda Conn Amstutz

Chapter **NINE**

September 8, 1995 – the wee hours

Bellevue

Later that evening (I had eaten and stayed up until the sun went down to get my internal clock set properly) I lay in bed thinking about the events of the day and then my mind wandered back.

I remembered the beginning years of Concepts, Inc. and the panicky times I wasn't sure if I would have enough cash to pay my employees and pay the bills too. For such a long time I was really "making it up as I was going along" until I had some experience upon which to fall back. Somehow I learned enough about advertising and about business to keep it going and to keep the money coming in – often just enough – there were times when I didn't take a pay check – quite a few of those in fact!

I have made the full circle – from beginning to the end – the end for me at least. It feels sad, like losing an old friend. Logically, I tell myself, this should be a happy time – I am moving on to the next phase of my life. Some of the time I can be logical.

I'm not sure I could ever have worked for someone else – I've not been able to "take direction" well. I'm not really a rebel, not exactly, but I tend to push back when someone tells me what to do rather than just going with the flow. Owning this agency has been good for me. I have had a chance to be creative – not that I can <u>draw</u> a straight line – my creativity is more in the area of ideas. No agency as small as mine can have a creative idea specialist – I also swept the floor and scrubbed the bathrooms, and kept books and paid bills and listened to the woes of my employees and my clients. I learned as I went along and I have had some lucky breaks and some good advisors and some great clients. But now I'm tired!

I. Am. Tired. I am sure some of my clients have noted a lack of enthusiasm which is surely the "kiss of
death" in a field where the young, sexy and enthusias-
tic reps take home all the bacon.

Either I don't have any ideas or the ones I have are
lackluster. I notice it now and can fake it for a bit but I
need to move on before everyone else notices that I am
not quite "with it." – quit while I am "on top." Selling a
small agency like mine is a tricky thing to do and I
know I am damned lucky to have found <u>anyone</u> interested in buying – let alone someone with Harry Lane's
experience.

Harry was the answer to my prayers. I never gave
much thought to whether or not prayers actually got
answered but there's no denying it. He is the answer to
mine, even though I don't remember asking. Have I
got a guardian angel watching over me?

Harry had worked in advertising as long as I have –
but always for someone else and he had wanted to be
his own boss. He did well enough to put some money
away and he can borrow some more. Now, he wanted
to buy "Concepts, Inc." from me – at a time when I re-

ally wanted to sell. While I spend this month in France, he will be sitting at my desk and getting to know my clients and employees and when I get back home we will settle the deal finally. It will work or it won't. Worst-case scenario would be that he would decide he hated it and I'd be back where I was - looking for a buyer!

Harry and I have worked together for the past three years doing promotion for The Hardy Group. He worked for Hardy and bought, first, print advertising, a catalog and then radio ads through Concepts. We have worked well together and The Hardy Group has become one of our best clients. To make a long story short, old Mr. Hardy's son graduated from college, and his dad hired him and gave poor loyal Harry his walking papers (well, he got a nice bonus too). The timing couldn't have been better – for me and for Harry. At first we both looked at this liaison with a jaundiced eye. We were afraid for a while it was too good to be true – but after we had done all our due diligence – it seemed to be workable for both of us. This trial period will tell us the final story, I think. I hope.

I am going to try to stay off the phone and let him find his own way for a while. It is hard though. Many of my clients are folks I have worked with for years and the temptation is to want to HELP – and I just mustn't. He seems to be doing fine with young Jeff Hardy – I was a bit worried about that – it would have been tough to lose that account but Jeff realizes he needs the experience Harry has, at least while Jeff is just getting his feet wet.

I am of two minds here: It is hard to let go and see someone else make their way in what has always been my job. But I really do want this to work, so that I am shed of the responsibility that has been keeping me from doing what I want to do, even though I have yet to determine what the heck that might be.

I am a bit past the age to become what I dreamed of as I was growing up.

I expected to be like my mother. Didn't all little girls in the 50s? We were perhaps the last generation of girls who actually could expect to follow in the footsteps of their stay-at-home-mom female role model – surely a false sense of direction but we had no reason yet to doubt it. My mom was a normal middle-class house-wife, married to a steady guy who went to work and came home at the end of the day to a home cooked meal, with a couple of (usually) well behaved children, two cars in the garage and maybe an occasional dinner out on special occasions. Yeah, right.

Growing up, I didn't question that when I reached the age of majority I too would have such a life. There didn't seem to be any way to avoid it. Everyone got married and had children – or if they didn't, well, they weren't "like me."

Actually, my first marriage pretty much looked like that from the curbside, never mind what happened behind my ruffled curtains on the windows. I certainly wanted it to be the model marriage, in a model home, with a model husband... How does a college girl, full of hormones, tell before it is too late, that a guy can't be satisfied without making his wife cry in pain? What makes a person need to hurt another to be feel good himself? To have to fool the world into thinking he is a nice guy, instead of him simply being a nice guy. And if it were happening to you, whom could you tell who would ever believe it?

I thought it was just going to have to be my cross to bear – my payment for the sin of making the precipitous decision to get married at the age of nineteen. I'd been antsy to get started with my life and thought I'd been preparing long enough. At first it was simply verbal abuse and I thought it must be my fault, something I had done wrong or was doing wrong. I would live with this mistake. Then he began to need to hurt me physically and I had to explore territory my mother never thought of traversing. Divorce had never been tried in my family – but try it I did... I never wanted to make my own living – I wanted to provide support to my husband while he did - but it was "do it myself" or go hungry.

Now, I was very lucky to have found someone, anyone at all, willing to buy an ad agency in a small town. Owning a small business can be a fairly masochistic exercise. You trade a lot of angst and financial insecurity for the questionable joy of having no one else making your decisions for you. It seemed to suit me. I survived twenty years of it – not, of course, without the help of loyal employees, good friends, good customers, and the bank. It has, much of the time, been fun; some of the time it has been satisfying, and at other times terrifying. It requires tons of energy, and if you're lucky your energy gets replaced. Lately, though, I have lost more than I gained and I am simply tired, burned out, spent. So I was going to sell Concepts, Inc. and someone else would have the worries and the satisfactions. I will have the time to do all the things that I have been procrastinating for the past too-busy twenty years!

Here I lay, snug in my narrow bed on this hilltop in rural France, thinking, "This is really happening! Soon I will free of this responsibility!

"I will have some real cash money to do something I want to do – maybe buy a sailboat – go fishing in South America – travel to the Far East – or buy a little house of my own in France…and I will have the time to enjoy those things. I have been cramming my pleasures into a weekend here and a holiday there – I can relax - not be in such a hurry. It's always seemed to me to be a waste of good fun to have to hurry to it and

from it, barely having sufficient time to savor the antic-
ipation and the afterglow. Even these month-long hia-
tuses seem too short."

The truth is, though, I have worked so much for so
long I am not sure I will know what to do with myself
when I don't have to "go to work". There have been
days when I went home earlier than my usual 8:00
p.m. and I was totally "at sea"! It was too early to eat
and I'd made no plans to go anywhere and I really
didn't know what to do with myself – seemed like
there ought to be something I "should" be doing...but
what? I need a life! – a life other than as president of
Concepts.

Such is the curse of the "over-employed"!

Right now I have a mission. If I could find Jean
Bertrand it would be a good beginning!

I must have fallen asleep, though I remember thinking sleep wasn't coming as easily as I had hoped – and
awakened to the black velvet darkness of this hilltop,
which is away from any artificial light. There was no
moon shining in the window but there seemed to be so
many more stars than I ever see at home.

Brring!

I could hear Clare's phone ringing in the distance. Her windows were open as were mine. It was too late for this to be good news, I suspect…

Shortly afterwards, she rapped on my front door, opened it, and called out, "Margaret? Are you awake? Margaret?"

"I am now." I came clomping down the stairs in my tee-shirt-cum-nightgown.

She was scowling, holding the extra phone, cord in hand, for me to plug into the jack upstairs. "Tell John that the time difference makes it six hours LATER here than in Ohio, please…"

I took it from her mumbling "Sorry," and she turned and padded back along the stone path to her house.

I plugged it in to the jack in the bedroom and do as I am told.

"John, it's two in the morning here. If you don't want me to be evicted you will NOT call in the middle of the night and wake Clare again. What's up?" I tried to sound slightly forgiving while I waited to see if this is

bad news or just a miscalculation of the time difference.

"Marg, I miss you. Aren't you glad to hear my voice?
Do you miss me too?"

I can hear the smile on his face – he really does love
me.

"I told Clare I was sorry for waking her, but now
that I have you on the phone, how are you? What have
you been doing? How was your flight? The train ride?
Do you really have to stay for three and a half more
weeks?"

"I'm fine and the trip was uneventful - I slept most of
the way. Clare met me at the train station in Bordeaux
and brought me here, and yes, of course, I am going to
stay. I want to stay. How are you?"

"Oh, I'm great – but I really miss you…"

"John, of course I miss you too, but the strangest
thing has happened… Clare has this new neighbor –
Jean – and they are interested in each other… seriously
interested, I think. But he has disappeared, just this
morning! We were supposed to go to Bergerac with
him today, and he wasn't there when we stopped after

our walk. Bizarrely, he left his door open – not un-locked, OPEN – and didn't take his cell phone with him or his car. He just is GONE!"

"I'm sure he is fine. Don't be a worry wart – and don't get involved in some local intrigue," he cautioned.

"But, John, you don't understand! He left his cell phone and his coffee was still warm when we got there. He simply vanished and there is no trace of him, though Conrad said he saw a small van…"

"Wait! Who's Conrad?"

"Oh, Conrad is Roberta's husband. They live down the lane – our closest neighbors – except, of course for Jean. Conrad was in the garden this morning and he saw the van come and go about the time Jean must have left."

"What van? Did he see Jean in the van?" John asked, adopting a reasonable even tone.

"Well, no, he wasn't exactly prepared to recall every detail. He just said he remembered seeing this little van – like a baker's delivery truck."

"I think you should just relax and enjoy your vacation and let Clare find her boyfriend – if he wants to be found" . Are you sure he does? Want to be found, I mean."

"Oh, I don't know".I answered in utter frustration,"I just know Clare is bereft. She has really grown fond of him and this all feels so...wrong, that's all!"

This conversation was acquiring a sort of stupid surreal character, maybe because of the distance, or the hour of the night or the fact that the whole situation IS surreal! Anyhow, I needed to get back to sleep – if I could get back to sleep – so I said, "John, of course I miss you, too. I am prepared to miss you for quite a while. And you know I'm not going to do anything stupid about this. Now I need to get back to bed. Why don't you write me a letter and then I will write you back when I get it? That way you won't have to apply for food stamps after you get your phone bill!" I tried to keep the tone in my voice light, but barely succeeded.

"OK, Sweetie, I'll let you go back to bed. I'm not much good at writing letters, but I'll try. I just want you to get home to be here with me. I'll call you on Sunday. It will have to be really early here – about midday there. Is that right? Six am here would be noon there? Have a nice time and please miss me a lot! I love you."

"Love you, too. I'll try to be here at noon on Sunday and I'll write back when I get your letter, I promise! Bye."

"Bye."

A click and suddenly it seemed so lonely here. A moment ago I was irritated that he didn't understand about Jean going missing and now, well…now, he was so far away and he was lonely too. My heart ached and I was wide-awake.

****

Frankly, I thought I would be glad to give this relationship with John a few weeks to settle while I was away. John's a great friend and I have grown very fond of him in the past year, but I'm afraid he is more serious than I'd like him to be. I need some space to get things organized at work and...and... I need a breather! He is an awfully good fellow and the death of his wife two years ago really devastated him. An aneurysm, I think. She wasn't sick. She was fine one day and gone the next. The suddenness really shook John to his core – and I think even, for a short time, it shook his faith.

John is the pastor of the Methodist church in a town about half an hour's drive south of Fairton where my advertising agency is located and where I live. We met about a year ago in an unusual way. He was on the wrong end of a bad debt I was trying to collect (my most-hated job function) and it wasn't really his fault the debt wasn't paid...not exactly. A small time pub-lisher (and big time charlatan) had hired my agency to broker the production of a membership directory for John's church.

Poor John, just getting over the loss of his wife and this bitch of an agency owner was making his life more difficult – well, this was one of the largest bad debts my small agency had ever incurred and I didn't think I could just forget it!

After some discussion I agreed to give the books to the church and write off the debt. John personally stuck labels on every book saying how generous we were and everyone was satisfied.

About a week after the resolution of this problem my phone rang and this dear man said to me (with, presumably, a perfectly straight face)"The Coalville Methodists can't reimburse you for your loss, but the least I can do is take you to dinner..."

I was once told that the finest compliment a dead spouse can be paid is for the widow or widower to want to be married again – it shows that marriage seemed a happy state to be in. I, now, get the distinct impression that's where John thinks this is going.

I, on the other hand, had pretty much decided I didn't need any man in my life. But to be cooperative, I agreed to have dinner but that was to be that!

Well, that wasn't that.

He was pleasant company – nothing thrilling, mind you, but just a genuinely nice person. He wasn't my type. He never was pushy exactly but he never gave up either. One evening he asked, "Why don't you want to go out with me? I keep asking and more often than not you say 'NO!' to me"

I simply told him (as gently as I could) that I wasn't interested in him in a romantic way and I hoped we could be friends but that was all. This man was different somehow. I simply couldn't find it within myself to hurt his feelings and I <u>did</u> want to be friends. I didn't know what was at work here, but I heard myself saying words that made more sense than the thoughts that were going on in my head. It was almost as if <u>I</u> were not the one talking. (Divine intervention?) And he kept calling me.

He was great for my ego. He sincerely thought I was a special person and I liked that. Who wouldn't like that? A person could get used to being "valued" - and he kept calling me.

But I didn't <u>need</u> a man to complicate my life. I was finally satisfied to be on my own. Plus, I was embroiled in selling my agency and there are too many changes going on - I couldn't deal with this right now.

It was good that I was going to be away for a while. What was I thinking? I am the last person whom anyone would expect to be a preacher's wife – or anybody's wife for that matter. I was set in my ways and much too used to my independence to change. No! It was good I was going to be here in France. I didn't need this constant "courting" thing. I needed to get my life together.

Chapter TEN

September 8, 1995, nearly dawn

Bellevue

I was really in trouble. I had had a little sleep and I was now wide-awake. At home it was past time to be getting up, so now I was back on Ohio time. Damn!

I turned on the light to read my book – hoping perhaps to get sleepy again – when just above my bed I spotted a behemoth of a spider, suspended in midair. Now, I am a self-sufficient, grown up, able-to-take-care-of-myself woman - except when it comes to spiders, and I had never seen the equal of this one! He (or she – but I somehow thought it must be a he) was fully four or five inches across – legs and all. And hairy – he was very hairy! There are centuries-old spider nests in the attics of these old stone buildings, and so long as they stay up there I am of the "live and let live" persuasion. But this guy had invaded MY territory and he was going to have to take the consequences. Slowly, so as not to alarm him and send him scrambling out of sight (a monster spider I can see is less scary than one who might be <u>anywhere</u>) I climbed out of bed and sneaked down the stairs to grab three things:

1. A can of bug killer

2. A paper towel

3. A fly swatter (in case the spray doesn't quite do the trick)

Back upstairs with my collection of weapons in hand, I moved oh-so-slowly closer. I didn't want to scare him back up and out of spray range. With mixed emotions about spraying the stuff right over my nice clean sheets, I blasted him with enough to dampen his prodigious fur and then everything happened quickly! He started to climb the thread of spider web on which he'd been suspended but just as suddenly lost steam and began to descend. I whipped the bedspread up (I didn't want him falling on MY sheets) and he reached the bed a split second later. With the paper towel, I flicked him to the floor and he limped drunkenly for a few paces and blat! I smashed him with the swatter (the ultimate indignity for a spider – to be swatted with a FLY swatter!).

It was over. I gingerly picked him up with the paper towel and carried him into the bathroom, and he met his final reward in a swirl of blue water.

I padded downstairs again to put away the poison spray and the swatter and to retrieve my notebook. If I was to make sense of things I needed to keep the facts and my questions organized. I was going to have Clare try to phone Thierry again and find out what he knew, and also ask him some questions about the story Jean told last night. Which boy had carried the message? What was the message about? Was this the situation that precipitated Thierry's father's death at the hands of the Germans?

And do we <u>know</u> it was the Germans who killed him?

I believed that there was something tying the story to Jean's disappearance.

He spoke of a refugee which Thierry's father was planning with the others to move to safety just before he was killed, and I had made a note to ask him who it was they were moving and what ultimately had happened to him. All this disappearance thing since then made me forget. Could that have been what was nagging me? I wonder who it might have been. It was a refugee – but from where?

I'll ask Clare later if she knows. If she doesn't, then I will move on to Thierry and Yves. Surely one of them will know.

Chapter ELEVEN

September 8, 1995, dawn

Bellevue

The sun came up and I was dressed and ready for my favorite day of the week to begin. Friday in Langnac is Market Day. It is the day - has been the day for centuries – literally centuries! – when the townspeople of little Langnac get together and shop and gossip and generally celebrate their connection with each other. This is a much more personal and effective and human method than cell phones and the Internet. Each family will send a representative or two, or many.

Fresh fruits and vegetables, meat, fish, cheese, olives, spices, wines, handmade pottery, clothing and household sundries - even corsets and toilet plungers - will be chosen and paid for.

Then the important business of the day can begin to be transacted. Around the market place are several *cafés* and it is there that the real business of the day is done. Over a *café petit crème* or *un verre de vin rouge* "Josette" will exchange the saga of the events of the week spent trying to keep up with the prodigious fig harvest for similar renditions of farm-keeping woes from "Marielle" who lives on the other side of Langnac, who will of course reciprocate with tales of spraying the grape vines to prevent whatever they spray to prevent. Politics and the price of gasoline will be discussed and derided. Even the comings and goings of men who are not the husbands of women who didn't think anyone was watching will be talked about.

And we could even learn something about the whereabouts of M. Bertrand at this market.

Clare was, typically, punctual – at 8:20 she was on her way to the garage. Simultaneously, Roberta walked up the drive, market basket in hand. We rode together into town, as parking, challenging on a "regular" day, is nearly impossible on Friday morning. No sense in taking two cars when one will do. Market baskets safely stored in the trunk, we were off down the steep drive to the main road into Langnac.

After the cursory "Good Morning" greetings Roberta queried, "Have you heard from Jean, Clare?"

"No, and I am worried something's happened to him...something bad. It is so unlike him to just disappear like this, with no warning. It is not as though he requires my permission to go somewhere, but he had invited Marg and me to go with him to Bergerac and was expecting us. He left his door <u>open,</u> for heaven's sake! His car and his cell phone are there...but you have heard all this. Oh Roberta, I am not making a mountain out of a molehill here. There is something wrong and we cannot even go to the gendarmes until tomorrow. I called them; it must be 48 hours before they consider that he is actually missing. And all this time, something is going on and we don't know what!"

"Who do you think it was in the little baker's van? Conrad is pretty sure he saw that van about the right time for it to have something to do with this... Does Jean have any friends who are bakers? "

Clare harrumphed. "Well, I have no idea. Aside from his boyhood buddies, Yves and Thierry, I haven't met any of his friends. Most of them are in Paris, I suppose. When he is here he is mostly working on the house."

I jumped in (trying to promote a little levity). "He is not working all the time – I saw him smooch the back of your neck before supper night before last. He's been doing some romancing as well as re-roofing, re-tiling and re— Oh, I don't know." I smiled encouragingly. "Seriously though, Roberta, who do you know who might be able to help us figure this out. You know everyone, at least all the anglophones."

"Have you talked with his two local friends?" Roberta asked.

"No, I tried calling both of them and had to leave messages on their phone answering machines. Neither has returned my call. When we get home from the market I will try again. Marg spoke with Yves, though.

He told her politely to butt out – that he was sure Jean was fine and we should not worry." Clare's shoulders slumped.

As we approached the village I told Roberta."Sounded for all the world as though he <u>knew</u> Jean was OK and wasn't telling us anything more."

The secret to finding a market day parking place quickly was three sets of eyes as we came down the main street, and NOT being too optimistic. There was always the odd chance that someone would be leaving just as we came – it happened, not often.

The lack of optimism manifested itself in the turn down the alley three blocks from the marketplace, where we can nearly always find a spot if Clare can wiggle this small car into it.

"See ya later," I say. Without discussion we would meet at 10:00 am at the *café*; the time and place were agreed years ago and hadn't changed.

My plan for the morning was to go first to the post office and buy some stamps, so that I could follow through on my promise to answer John's letter and perhaps make some sense for him out of events of the past couple of days in written form. Then I'd pop into the bakery - because as good as the bread is at the market, I think the bread at the *boulangerie* by the post office is the better! It has crust not for those with delicate bridgework, baked in a wood-burning oven and has a wonderful sour yeasty aroma and taste. I tease my friends on the faddish low carbohydrate diets by telling them I fly 8000 miles (round trip) each year to eat this bread while they are eschewing bread altogether!

This little shop has seen a recent change of ownership that has given me hope for the future of commerce in this tiny town – the old baker and his wife, who minded the shop selling the baker's nights work, retired and sold the business – storefront, ovens in the basement, living quarters above and all – to a delightful young couple who have changed nothing except the face behind the counter.

Among the choices there was a skinny, short, one-person loaf called *ficelle*, which I always bought.

Also, making my decision more difficult, there are *baguettes* which are about twice as long and also skinny: *bâtards*, which are larger, fatter loaves; *pain de mais* (bread made with corn meal); *pain complet* (whole grain bread); tempting little *quiches* incorporating leeks, mushrooms, sardines, and/or Emmenthal cheese; *éclairs*; tarts of *citron* (lemon), strawberries, or raspberries; luscious *Napoleons*; and – of course – flaky, light, crusty, brown *croissants* – of which I always take two, please. (One of these won't make it home!)

Exhibiting steely self control, I left with two *croissants* and a *ficelle*. Only two *croissants* and a *ficelle*!

Now I got to the business of marketing – a serious one. I walked through the produce section and looked at fruits and vegetables. Such fruit! A French housewife from Langnac wouldn't give a second glance to the produce found in most U.S. supermarkets – here I saw each   uniformly-sized strawberry placed with the pointy end going in the same oblique direction in the little wooden box. <u>These</u> berries wouldn't make it in a US supermarket either – as they are ripe – perfectly ripe today – picked last night or this morning before dawn – and won't be good tomorrow. But, today! Oh! Today they will fill your mouth with real strawberry flavor as if you had picked them in the field and popped it still warm from the sun into your mouth (not as though they had been picked green because they needed three days in a shipping container and two at the wholesaler's). The woman I bought my strawberries from grew these berries herself and picked them this morning.

As I made this comparison, I popped one of these succulent little gems in my mouth.

The chickens are like that too. The old man who sells the fresh killed birds had a line of perhaps a dozen men and women waiting to have him choose their bird personally depending upon what they proposed to do with it. It might be for a stew, or to stuff with truffled rice stuffing; for the woman and her husband or the two of them and three voracious adolescent children... But it must be discussed and he had just the bird for each preparation. And other alternatives were available as well: Guinea fowl; quail; and *rillettes*. His are in such demand. He cut a slice from the two foot long loaf of bits and pieces of poultry parts held fast with chicken fat and seasoned very delicately with sage and thyme.

" *Une tranche de rillettes, s'il vous plaît.*"[a slice of the *rillettes*, please]I said in my best French to the kind man when it was finally my turn; a small hunk of chickeny delight to spread on a slice of toasted bread to accompany my aperitif. I also bought a bird – the breast and thighs I would separate and stow in the freezer and the rest of the bird would make a lovely stock – I have found I cannot cook without chicken stock and keep cubes of it frozen for use at a moment's notice. The double breast would be good if I have company for supper and the thighs would each make a nice supper for me alone. And these parts taste like real chicken - we don't know, in the U.S., this real authentic farm-raised chicken flavor.

A small battered Plexiglas cooler across the aisle from the stand which sold olives and spices holds goat cheeses of varying ages – and I adored them all, as well as the girl who made them. To watch her handle the individual pieces is to begin to understand what made food shopping here so satisfying. She had pride in each piece she sells. She made them.(Well, she and the goats.) She lifted the fresh ones carefully, as they are crumbly and still drip whey. Then she wraps three little slightly aged tiny round *cabecous* for me – they are yummy dusted with some breadcrumbs and heated to dress a salad (like the one we had yesterday) of frisee lettuce which then needs only a drizzle of olive oil to be just right.

I am trying not to get carried away and buy too much – after all there is only me to eat these treasures.

I will buy a few vegetables and then I will quit and head for the *café*. Here in this market the carrots are big and fat. At home "big and fat" would signal a harsh bitter tasting stringy old carrot. Not so here. These carrots are sweet and delicate and delicious and one of them is more than I can eat at one sitting! More than once I have cooked a carrot for my supper – just one and nothing else! I cut it in bite-sized chunks and sauté it with a clove or two of garlic and at the end add a teaspoon or so of peppery fresh olive oil – simple and delicious. So I bought a couple carrots and too many *haricots verts* (lovely uniformly skinny green beans). I bought too many because I never can remember how to say "a quarter of a kilo" – so I bought a *demi-kilo*, which was twice what I needed. I would have to look it up again when I got back to my French-English dictionary.

Last but not least: my Friday lunch. It wasn't lunchtime yet but by the time I got home it surely would be close – and here was the rotisserie wagon.

This fellow got to the market square early on Friday with his trailer with a gas-fired rotisserie. Six or seven 5 foot long skewers hung horizontally, one above the other would turn slowly. He roasted ducks, capons, chickens, *coquelets* (very small chickens) and quails. The juice from the birds on the top skewer would drip on and blend with the next and so on dripping down into the tray at the bottom in which he had strategically positioned slices of onions, potatoes, garlic, butter and seasonings. Mesmerized, I followed a drip of duck juice which blended with the chicken and finally the quail and fell into the bath of oniony seasoned "sauce" he scooped up a ladle full and poured it over the topmost birds and it took another journey gathering more and more flavor as the roasting process continued. The aroma as I approached my turn in the line is making my mouth water. Lunchtime couldn't come soon enough!

I said to the short plump moustachioed Frenchman *"Une petit caille, s'il vous plâit,"* he asked me, *"Avec jus?"*, as he forked my little quail into the waxed paper/foil bag. Who in their right mind would turn down a ladle of <u>that</u> sauce?

"Oui!" I answered rolling my eyes enthusiastically, paid him and hurried off to the *café*. By now, it was (typically) after ten o'clock.

The *café* was full. Clare and Roberta have saved a chair for me and as I sat, shoe-horned between Clare and a woman I have not yet met who is speaking English with a German or perhaps Dutch accent, the taller of the two young waiters walked over and says, *"Madame?"*

"Café, grande crème, s'il vous plâit," I replied, and he hurried off. I threw some change into the ashtray, along with payments from the others to cover the cost of the coffee and something for the young server who

looked cute in his black vest with the long white apron tied round his waist. Now the gossip could begin in earnest...

Clare didn't ask about Jean, as no one, except Roberta, with whom we were sitting even knew him. However, as we caught up on local news, across the street beside a market stand selling shoes, Yves stood in deep consultation with a man in a dark suit. Was he the priest? Soon another, more casually dressed, man walked up and said something to the two of them and all three left together, walking in the direction of the church.

Puzzled, I made a mental note of it.

Clare, Roberta and I shortly made for the car and headed home. A good thing too! No sooner had we arrived at Bellevue (we were standing in the middle of the driveway dividing a container of strawberries, as none of us wanted more of them than we could eat before they spoiled) than the orange and purple FedEx truck came up the lane! I asked the driver to wait, opened the cardboard envelope, quickly read over and signed the contract and filled out new paperwork, handing him some euros and sending it back the same way it came. I was glad to have that finished and on its way back to Harry.

He'd be happy.

Chapter TWELVE

Early Spring 1941

Outside of Langnac, southwest France

Sandrine Duranthon

Sandrine lay cocooned in the warm goose feather filled bed she shared with Roland. Soon her day would begin with reviving the fire in the stove then venturing out into the frosty morning, frozen gravel crunching beneath her wooden clogs as the sun was just beginning to color the eastern sky. First, she would walk to the pump for a bucket of water for washing and to make one cup of "ersatz coffee" (not real coffee, a roasted barley mixture - there was no more coffee, but this drink at least would be hot).

Just for this one moment, she let thoughts of Roland fill her head and conjured, from her memory, the comfort of his warm body next to her. She smelled his scent on the sheet and closed her eyes, remembering the last time they were together. Was it last week, or last month? The world had become such a confusion of fear and worry and work and loneliness and this empty bed. Roland had been gone since just after dark last night and wouldn't be home until mid-day. He would sleep then for an hour or two and then begin the work on the field by the road so that the corn will be planted there about the same time as the neighbors'. No one would note his absence from the fields of the past few days. She hoped.

Robert and Thierry had been working hard each day after school to fill in where Roland's absence might create questions. So far, so good.

Now, Sandrine sat on the edge of the bed, slid her feet, warm from beneath the covers, into socks of wool and her old fashioned wooden clogs and wrapped a worn woollen shawl around her shoulders, ready to make the trek from the front door to the barn. There, in the dim light, she grabbed an apron and filled the pockets with rough-ground corn from a sack by the door on her way out. It was breakfast for the hens, Rosanne and Hillarie, and their broods, and that loud and rowdy Raphael who would soon be crowing the announcement of the advent of this day at the top of his lungs.

Her apron pocket upon her return to the kitchen would have a couple of eggs for the boys' breakfast, probably the best meal of the day for them, perhaps the only one.

"As frightening a time as this is," Sandrine prays, trying to find something to thank God for in this horrid war, "It could be so much worse. My sons are here. Some neighbors' sons aren't. We have enough to eat – barely – and a bit to share with those fleeing and those fighting the Bosch. God bless them…and protect my little family, please.

"Roland is a good man; he could do no less than to help those who are actively fighting the Germans. At least, so far, he isn't fighting them himself. A bullet hitting him now would be accidental, not shot in retaliation for one he shot at them. And his conscience won't carry the burden of killing. Who would have thought these would be things for which I would be thanking You?"

"The two Douchet boys, from the next hamlet, have been conscripted to labor in the German factories - *"Service du Travail Obligatiore"* – and supposedly, in exchange, two prisoners will come home from the prisoner of war camps, but who will know if the bargain will be completed. All they do is take, the damned Germans: take our food, take our animals, take our men – even some single women have been taken. There is nothing left to take in this village! All the young men are gone and the harvest from last year is gone also. God , only you know what we will eat this year. *Oh, Mon Dieu,* I feel so old! What happened to the plans I made as a girl? I knew Roland would be my life even then but this surely is not the life I had imagined for us… Lord, please, protect us all!"

Raphael, the rooster, heralded the dawn and jerked Sandrine from her prayerful contemplations; she scattered corn for him and for his small harem and their offspring. Sandrine counts herself lucky to have him and his family. Some of her neighbors are not so fortunate. The ration cards do no one any good when there is nothing to buy! There was no coffee, real or otherwise, to replace the bitter stuff that she would drink this morning; there wasn't any sugar to sweeten it and yesterday there was no bread left when she got to the baker's at nine in the morning. Thank God, last fall she gathered chestnuts to grind. At least there would be some heavy moist homemade bread from that after she got her outdoor chores done and gathered enough wood for a fire in the bread oven, unlike those who lived in the village and had no access to anything to burn for warmth!

Another thankful prayer went up from Sandrine to her familiar God.

"I am lucky", she prays, "because the hardship we face has brought me closer to You. I feel it's necessary to talk with You more often than in times of peace. I recognize the simple gifts because of the absence of plenty – another blessing. *Alors!*" Something moved in the corner of the empty horse's stall.

"*Ah, mon cher!* It is you! You startled me!"

---

* * * *

Roland Duranthon

Roland crossed the straw-littered space to embrace his wife. It seemed so much more imperative to touch, to kiss, to hold her. He didn't want to speak of it, but he knows that each time literally could be the last and he must savor this intimate moment. She felt so small, but he knew her strength, her simple daily courage as she tried to make this time of war a time of growth and peace for her family when evil flourished in this part of "Independent France". Hatred for the Germans, their Vichy government puppets, and for those neighbors who would sell their souls for a bit of black market booty – information sold for a pack of cigarettes puts a villager's son, a *resistante*, into the ranks of the "deported" or worse. Roland had heard gossip, tales so depraved he was not inclined to believe them, much less share them with Sandrine, about what "deported" meant. And though he did not share these tales with her, somehow, on some level, she knew too. She maintained her love of country in the face of Marschal Petain's alliance with that devil-incarnate, Hitler. She can (and therefore Roland can) believe that this war will end and France will again become the place they loved as children. She is, for him, the source of continuity, strength and his reason for being. But at this moment he has brought the danger he lives with every day into the sanctuary which is their barn – their home. What could he do?

There is more movement in the dark corner. What? A girl. Her frightened eyes told it all. She was young - almost as young as Sandrine and Roland's two boys – but she is alone and her stringy hair, dirty face and torn clothing suggested she had been running for longer than just today.

"Rol-" Sandrine begins.

"Shhh! No names! The less she knows, the safer we are and she is," Roland hisses.

"Who is she?"

"Her parents were taken – put on a train bound for Germany – last week, I think. Somehow she'd got separated and *Père* Joseph found her and kept her hidden in Siorac. We have to make some papers for her and get her to my brother in Bergerac and thence to the Spanish border.

"I am sorry, my love, but for now she must stay here while I work on finding her an identity and while she gets some rest. It is an arduous journey to the border and she needs something to eat. What do we have that we could share? Tonight I will take her to Pierre."

Sandrine sighs. "This girl will eat the eggs I gathered for the boys. She will need them more than they, the poor child. Does she have any more clothes? It will be cold in the mountains."

The child looked with large brown eyes from one of them to the other. Perhaps she spoke no French? What experiences awaited this young girl – her parents lost, the journey with strangers to a land unknown to her and a future of…what?

"*Est-elle juive*?" (Is she a Jew?)

Roland nodded.

Sandrine thinks, "She is better off freezing to death in the mountains than here if she is caught by the Germans! Dear God, protect this child." But she says nothing aloud.

She walks across the stall, takes the trembling girl in her arms and holds her close – and she prays again. This time her prayer is about hope that there would be someone to embrace her boys as she does this girl, should the worst happen to her and to Roland. This girl's presence could easily cause that eventuality, but what could they do? Turn this child away? "Oh, *mon Dieu*, the choices we must make…" She sighs.

She hugs her tighter then abruptly lets her go and leaves the barn to cobble together some breakfast for this child and to find something for her own boys.

Roland rides away on the bicycle to meet his contact who might be able to provide the girl with identification, which would convince a German border guard she posed no threat to "the fatherland".

Left alone in the barn, the young refugee girl wrapped herself in the prickly horsehair-covered blanket Roland has provided and made herself a nest in the hay, on the side opposite the door so that she might hear a German patrol entering before they saw her – she hopes. She closed her eyes not able to remember the last time she slept.

* * * *

Sandrine, having fed her boys their least favorite – the heels of last week's chestnut bread – for their breakfast and sent them upstairs to get ready for school, enters the barn once more.

"Petite chère." Sandrine realizes she doesn't know the child's name. *"Petit déjeuner pour toi..."*

The girl wakes with a start. What had she heard? Oh, it is just the woman of the kind eyes and warm embrace. Her own French is stilted but she can recognize the smell of breakfast and timidly she lifts her head over the top of the hay and addresses the woman.

"Madame? Ooo, Merci!"

Sandrine offers the plate of food and mug of warm milk she has brought.

"Merci" the child repeats, wide-eyed and timidly.

Sandrine sits on a three-legged stool, thinking, and watches as the girl devours the food she has brought, "I wonder when she last ate, probably before her parents were taken, unless *Père* Joseph found something for her in Siorac. By the way she is devouring this though, I suspect not much!"

"Do you speak French"? Sandrine asks the girl.

"*Oui, Madame*, et Yiddish…"

"Where do you come from?"

Haltingly, she answered, "Liège –in Belgium. My father has a gallery for art there and my mother, she is a professor of music at the university. She is a cellist.

They are both working now in a camp in Germany but, after the war…"

Sandrine reaches for the girls shaking hand and warms it in her own. She is not as cold as she is tired and terrified.

"Oh, my dear God, protect this child," Sandrine silently prays, "she knows where her parents are and she is being so brave. Keep her safe until she gets to the sanctuary of Spain." And then what?

Sandrine takes the dish and mug and the girls hand and leads her to the house. She is nearly large enough to wear some of Sandrine's clothing and she will need warmth going over the mountains. She wears sturdy enough shoes, but a sweater and some sort of coat…

⁂

✶✶✶✶

Annaliesa

She returned again to the barn, with a sweater and some itchy woollen pants, and burrowed into the straw again, pulling the rough blanket over herself.

Slowly, she began to feel better for the warm clothes and the eggs and hard toasted bread she had been given. She wondered if now were the time to part with her father's last "treasure".

Her papa had hurriedly packed some things from their fine house in Liège. "Small, portable treasures" he had called them. They were, she thought at first, the things he held most dear. Soon, she learned otherwise. He had traded the onyx and gold signet ring for their train tickets bound for Bordeaux, then the ornate silver salver for a couple of stale sandwiches. Then, when the German soldiers had closed in on them, her dear papa had hidden her in the trunk on the ramp by the train station, and as *Pére* Joseph had told her that he bravely marched arm in arm with her frightened mother, away from her, like a bird feigning a broken wing, drawing attention away from its nest. But before he kissed her goodbye, he had slipped into her hand the small painting of the Virgin Mary – not as a French father might have, so that the holy Virgin might protect his daughter, but with instructions to find someone who would buy it should she need money to facilitate her safety.

She knew only that the painter was a Renaissance master and that the painting was valuable. Andrea di Verrochio, a teacher of the great Leonardo, had painted it early in the 15th century. It was small and dark. The woman, Mary, wore a cloak of clearest blue and a sad expression lingered in her eyes. Papa had said to find a church or an art dealer and sell it when she ran out of the coins he had also given her...could she trust the man who brought her here? Or the woman? Would they know someone in this village to buy it? Surely they could not afford it. Theirs was a poor farm, shabby. She had seen only one cow and a few skinny chickens. So who then, was there to buy her "small portable treasure"?

She had heard them talking about the mountains, and Spain... No one had asked her where she wanted to go. Not that she would have known what to say if they had. But her papa always included her in family decisions. He treated her as though she had a good mind, and she resented being trundled by these strangers from one place to the next: the church in Siorac, now to this barn and then to "the mountains" and eventually to Spain, without so much as a care for what she wanted.

Then she wondered how her parents would find her when they were done working in Germany? Had these people thought that far? She was not, after all, a child any longer. At twelve, she was old enough to think for herself.

A noise! She shrunk into the corner, trying to become invisible in the murky light of the barn. The door slid open and for a moment she was blinded by the glare. Then she saw a boy, younger than she, but not much. He was slight of build and sandy haired and wore a dark wool coat and wooden clog shoes. He went to the stall next to hers, retrieved a rusty bicycle and walked it out, closing the barn door behind him, oblivious to her presence. She let out the breath she had been holding, realizing at once that should someone ask her what she would choose to do, she would have no idea in the world what to answer. Papa had told her to stay away from the German soldiers and beyond that she had no plan... So she might as well go to the mountains and then to Spain – to safety in Spain – as she was told.

Safety? She wondered if she would ever feel safe again…

Chapter THIRTEEN

Sunday morning, early Spring 1941
Langnac, *Église* du Notre Dame

Sandrine Duranthon

In rows of chairs in the back of the crowded church sat the parents of the three boys, Sandrine, and her friends who had been close since their childhood. They had all heard from their own parents of the war of their parents' youth but this, their own experience, was still surreal to them. Sandrine, the most devout of the six of them, knelt on the cushion before her, eyes closed, and prayed her own prayer as the priest prattled on in Latin. The fact that she couldn't understand him was a relief to her as she had her own issues to silently discuss and entreat her very familiar God about, and she didn't need distraction.

"Please protect Roland as he, Arnauld and Louis make plans for the Jewish child, keep my boys from harm and help me to somehow find enough for us to eat this week…and next."

She looked at her husband, Roland, who was here mostly for the sake of appearance. It would be spoken about in the town if he didn't show up at mass on a Sunday morning, but he was also here because it provided an innocent forum for him to speak with his friends. There was no suspicion of ulterior motives for their meeting if it was held in this place at this time. The meeting was imperative too, he had told her, as the identification papers for the Jewish child had taken longer to be created than they had hoped. The child had been in the hidden now for three days, a dangerous if not disastrous situation that could not continue.

Each day added to the danger, both for the child and for those who sheltered her.

"… And, Holy Father, please protect this poor girl as she journeys to Spain."

Roland had hoped that Louis or Arnauld had the documents or at least knew they were prepared so that the journey to Bergerac and then to the Spanish border could begin. His head bowed, Sandrine heard him as he whispered to Louis beside him to the left, "Have we got the documents?"

"No, alas, they should be ready by tonight, or so I am told. But then I have been told this for three days! Is she ready to travel? Your brother is alerted?" Arnauld asked.

"Yes, and I would like to see this situation over. Nowhere is a safe place to store this type of contraband!" He momentarily glanced at her. "We are taking a terrible risk."

Sandrine was sure that Arnauld knew this already. "I will go this time. It's too dangerous for you to be seen there another day. My boys can do the planting for me this afternoon. I just want this to be finished," Roland concluded, his voice firm.

Sandrine was appreciative that Roland, Arnauld and Louis worked as an independent cell, not in the larger "*route*" of the *Maquis*. It was in some ways more difficult than it would be with more help and more people with whom to share the responsibilities but, there was much less danger of discovery. If the three friends told no one else of their plans, then there would be no one to betray them to the Germans.

Langnac was not officially "occupied" as a town – there were no German soldiers billeted in the town (they slept in the hamlet of Siorac just beyond the Duranthons' farm where there was a railway station), but their presence was constant and unavoidable. The men ate in the small café on the square and flirted with the younger, and sometimes the older, women of Langnac. They rode at all hours through the streets, both on motorcycles and in the trucks which were easy to identify, as there was little or no gasoline for the locals. If you heard a truck, it was usually German.

The mayor of Langnac worked with the German commander in Siorac to keep order. His was an unenviable position – suspected by both the people of his own village and by the Germans.

Now, he sat just two rows of chairs in front of Sandrine. So when the priest was quiet, so must the three men in her row be.

Sandrine recognized the Latin phrases that signalled that they approached the end of the mass and heard Arnauld volunteer, "I will come by after dark and take the girl to your brother, if you get the documents - or even if you do not."

Louis and Arnauld leaned forward to see Roland nodding his assent, thereby making further words unnecessary.

Roland had told Sandrine that Arnauld had been in contact with the forger of identification papers for each of the past three days and did not like the job one bit. No one but his two old friends could be truly trusted, and as this damned war continued he became more and more suspicious.

The supplies of gasoline were gone for all practical purposes, unless you were German, of course, and food was becoming increasingly scarce. She knew her friend Louis would have given a lot for a cup of real coffee. But there are those, perhaps even some in this town, who would give the Germans Louis himself for a taste of the real stuff, or for news of the whereabouts of a son, or to keep a German officer from his daughter.

There was no night when Roland's sleep was untroubled or his daytime activities were not carefully arranged to look innocent – even if they were innocent!

And the past three days had not been innocent.

Their friend Arnauld had ridden his bicycle to Challerville, six kilometres away, each day to fetch the papers and they had not been ready – and each day there was a new reason. Roland had told her that the girl should be moved tonight even with no papers. It was simply too dangerous to keep her just under the noses of the Nazis. Surely they would be killed, not to mention the girl, but also if connections could be made, Arnauld and Louis and their wives and children could be also targets of German "discipline".

The Germans usually said, "Others must be shown the price for duplicity and subversion." Though how could anyone consider a child a threat? Where did this hatred arise from? What possible harm could this girl do to anyone?

The Germans' answer was as simple, of course, as it was without merit. "She was a Jew."

The priest was making the blessing on his flock, and the mass and the "meeting" were ended. Smiles all around and cheek kisses for friends and shortly everyone would be headed for their homes and a meal.

Louis, doing his job as *sacristain*, went to the back to open the doors, and the people all departed, stopping outside to chat with their friends and neighbors seen just this one day each week.

---

* * * *

The three boys, Thierry, Yves and Jean, had formed a knot in the yard and, as their parents were distracted by greetings from acquaintances, were cooking something up – as they seemed always to be doing.

"No, I cannot tell you, just yet anyway. I have to find your papa, Yves," Thierry Duranthon whispered to his two friends. "I will tell you later. Right now, I have to go. But you must wait here!" It was an order.

He slid the brown paper "something" from the handlebars of his bicycle in a deft and fluid motion – behind his back – and slid the narrow package up his sweater's frayed sleeve. Quickly, he walked back up the steps and into the church.

The other two boys looked at each other, wondering what their friend had got himself into this time. Less than ten minutes later, he emerged from the front of the church and fairly skipped down the steps, high color on his face and a smile a mile wide showing gaps in his teeth where the new grown up teeth hadn't yet come in.

Thierry hoisted the bicycle up and, while the other two boys stood together, effectively making a fence between the after-mass crowd, the Germans and the bicycle, Thierry silently slipped something into the handlebar with no grip. Gracefully, he swung his leg over the seat and waved to his friends, laughing, as he rode down the lane toward the nearby village of Siorac. He pedalled, joyfully, across the boundary between their town, seemingly overrun if not formally occupied by the German Army, past the checkpoint and into *Vichy* France, governed by the régime of General Petain to the hamlet where his grandmother and parents lived and where their barn hid the girl with the dark eyes...

Linda Conn Amstutz

Chapter FOURTEEN

September 8, 1995, late evening

Bellevue

Margaret

I had been looking at this problem as though it were something I'd never encountered before, but actually it had many similarities to my advertising business. A client has a product to sell and we are hired to find a way to do it. In this case, my friend has a problem and she has asked me to help her to solve it. Well, she didn't really ask, but then, some clients don't exactly say the words "Help me" either.

My listening skills and problem solving skills should translate – at least to some extent – and so far I have made a list of what we know and discovered that we don't know much.

Jean's story about the boys during the war is still prickling my mind and I am certain on some level that therein lies the answer, or at least the beginning of the trail. It never works to skip steps, though, so first thing tomorrow morning Clare and I will go to the *gendarmerie* and make an official report of Jean Bertrand as a missing person. I wonder if Clare has a photo of him. That will also go on my list.

I would have liked to have been near enough to hear what the priest, the other man and Yves were talking about this morning at the market. Maybe nothing of important, but it looked more like "something" to me. And I am also curious about the fact Yves didn't mention the church's fortifications. Why did Jean disappear just now? It can't have had anything to do with my arrival, but something caused it to happen at this point in time? Hmmm…another item for the list.

* * * *

September 9, 1995, morning

Gendarmerie, Langnac

Clare shot a panicked look at me before getting out of the car and asked, "Should we be doing this?"

"I know what you're feeling, Clare, but we need to do this. Perhaps the police will know something we don't – like who owns the white van, or something. Let's go in and get it over with." I spoke with more optimism than I felt.

We got out of the car and walked into the building made of brick and stone. There was a small vestibule and a window of very thick glass to the right of the door, a small metal vent to allow sound to enter (but presumably no bullets?). No one was behind the window but in answer to some silent signal of our arrival, a young woman in dark blue uniform pants, a white shirt with sewn-in creases and a black plastic name badge with the letters SONIA DOUCHET routed in it.

She greeted us in French (I expected something else?) and Clare answered, explaining that we were here because we were concerned about the disappearance of her neighbor. The young woman asked us to come in, through the door, which she unlocked with a key from the large ring fastened to her belt. I was left to presume she found us less than threatening.

We followed her to a rather large office with several desks, only one of which had a computer on it. She indicated that we should sit and dragged a spare plastic stacking chair so there was a place for each of us to do that. Then she drew up a rolling stool and sat herself behind the desk with the computer. She spoke directly to Clare and asked the missing man's name – *prenom* and family name – then asked his age and for a physical description. And did she have a photo?

Clare dug in her bag and found a small silver frame with a snapshot of her and Jean smiling for their photographer with Jean's heliotrope colored front door shutters in the background.

The list of questions went on and she entered all the information about the warm coffee, cell phone, white van, etc., into the computer. I understood most of what she asked and all of Clare's answers. It is much easier to understand than to speak, and I had anticipated what she had wanted to know. Then the gendarme asked me if I had anything to add to the report.

"*Non, desolée.*"

I really didn't know much more than Clare had already been over with her, except that Yves might know something but decided to keep that to myself...

(Yves might be more likely to tell Clare something than the police!) So I said I didn't really have anything to add.

She handed Clare a card with her name and several phone numbers on it and we walked back to the locked door, which she opened, before we returned to Clare's car.

Clare got in and lay her head back against the headrest, heaving a huge sigh. This had been a difficult time for her – even more difficult than I had imagined, perhaps. I suggested we stop at the *café* and perhaps emulate the old French farmers and have *un verre de vin rouge* to start our day, and we did.

We stopped by the church before going home and nosed around until we found Yves in the garden. He smiled when he saw Clare then gave me an odd look which I couldn't identify, finally giving me also his best friendly smile. Clare officially introduced me and he gave her the requisite two cheek kisses and shook my hand formally. Maybe next time he'll give me the friendly kisses also. Third time's a charm!

This conversation we carried on in English – for my benefit, I suppose.

Yves casually asked, "Have you heard from Jean?" and, of course Clare answered in the negative. She then told him that we had just been to the *gendarmes* to make an official report of his disappearance.

He seemed surprised, looking around as if to see if anyone had heard the question and something else I couldn't put my finger on. Then he casually put a hand in one pocket and said, "Don't you think that is a bit drastic? He will probably come home any time and be irked at having to make explanations of his whereabouts."

"No I don't think it is at all drastic! I think if he wanted for me not to be worried he should have given some explanation of his absence especially since we had plans for the morning. I am sincerely concerned for his welfare and if the police can help I want their help."

I was proud of Clare – she stood her ground.

She continued. "I am curious why you, as his friend, are not concerned. Do you know something I don't?" [I think "You GO, girl!"] "I have not known him as long as you, surely, but this seems to me to be out of character for him. Do you disagree?"

"*Chère* Clare, I am sorry you are worried. I am certain he didn't mean for you to be troubled over this. I have known Jean forever, it seems, but have not seen him often for many years until he moved into the house near to yours last autumn. I am sure he has some good reason to be gone and I hope especially for your sake, he will be home soon. Please forgive me if I was unsympathetic."

He walked up to Clare and put his arm around her shoulder whereupon she dissolved into tears. Silently, he finished the embrace and held her until she stopped sobbing and hiccuped a couple of times, wiped her eyes and nose on the handkerchief he proffered.

"I hope you are right." Taking a step back, she asked, "Yves, if you aren't in the middle of something – would you have time to show me the organ? Marg said you were playing it. I didn't know the installation was complete!"

She winked at me as Yves agreed then turned and walked down the path to the church door.

"I'd love to show you. There are still some details of the pipes needing to be worked out – but it sounds glorious, and I am enjoying it at least as much as M. de Rastignac. The poor man has been in Paris for the past two weeks and hasn't played it himself since all the pipes were connected!"

He opened the back door with a key almost as big as his hand and the hinges screeeeeked like a cellar door in a B-horror film. That was my cue.

"Yves, does this church have any place to hide. I mean if the marauding English, for example, came pillaging through the countryside – would the lord and the villagers have hidden in the chateau or would they have sought a place where they would be less likely to be found?"

He looked directly at Clare and laughed. "Clare, have you been teaching history again? Yes, Margaret – as a matter of fact - the fortifications in this church have caused a problem just recently with the placement of the pipes for this organ. Let me show you... just here," (he gestured at the hallway to the right), "on the other side of that wall was the planned position of the largest pipes, but the reverberations from the hollow space hidden behind the wall made an awful sound and we had to re-position them to the other side of the chancel. We knew of a couple of places where there were double walls - both were in the dome – but this place was a surprise, even to me. My papa did not know, or if he did, he didn't tell me before he died. And I thought he'd told me everything about this place!"

I surreptitiously shot a satisfied grin at Clare and asked Yves, "Could we look? I'd love to see where they hid. Or is it too much trouble?"

He stopped and looked around at us. "I can show you the entrance to the space in the dome. Follow me!" He walked into the apse and up some steps I hadn't seen before – hidden behind a wooden screen. Moving a wooden panel, and he was GONE! A couple of seconds later he peeked around the panel, a big smile on his face. "This way, ladies…"

Taking a cigarette lighter out of his pocket, he lit a wooden torch, the end wrapped in cloth, and feeling like we were in a scene from "The Mummy's Tomb", we followed him up the narrow stone stairway curving to our left around the shape of the dome. I would not have liked to spend any time in this "safe" place – preferring to take my chances with the marauders rather than the millions of spider webs in here, but Yves was burning most of the webs away with the torch. I suppose he was scaring their spinners into the crevices between the stones…for a while anyhow. I wanted OUT of here, but I had asked him to show us and now I was stuck. For how long, I wasn't sure.

When we arrived at what must have been the top of the dome there was a space nearly high enough to stand in and a flat area underfoot maybe eight feet in diameter. Above our heads was the roof of the dome and light filtered through several holes – horizontal slits through which the light shone – but rain would not come in, unless it was blowing sideways.

I asked Yves, "Does this place go all the way around the dome?" Not sure I wanted to have to actually go all the way around. His word would be good enough for me. Then we could get the hell out of this creepy place and its too-close walls and eight-legged residents.

"No", he answered. "The end of this side is just there." He gestured ahead of us. [Oh thank God!] "There are a couple of other places where the walls are hollow and a few people could stay for a very short time in the case of a sudden emergency. But this is the largest [The largest? Yeeks!]

Clare (thankfully) chimed in, "I think we have seen enough. Marg has the general idea and she can see that a person would have to be seriously scared to want to be in this place. The days of the Hundred Years' War and after were quite unpleasant, but the town survived and here we are!"

By now we had turned around and were descending the narrow stairway into the larger area and would soon be out. I could actually breathe again!

When we reached the bottom of the steps Clare turned to Yves and, a serious look on her face, she asked, "Yves, do you know where Jean is?".

He studied her for a long moment and took a deep and slow breath.

"Yes, I do. But you must trust me, and you must not worry for him. He is safe and he is, I am sure, concerned for your feelings, but you must trust me..."

"But where... Why?"

"Not now, Clare, and not here...but soon." Yves tried to assure her.

We left the churchyard, but not before passing by a gap between the house where Yves lived and the church to see a small white van, like a baker might use for his deliveries, parked close under a large vine covered arbor.

Linda Conn Amstutz

Chapter FIFTEEN

Spring, 1941, Sunday morning early

Thierry rode swiftly, his heart pounding, his eyes watering and his cheeks burning in the chill spring air. Finally, he was really doing something to help. For so long he had watched his Papa leave after the lights were all out at night and when his *Maman* thought he and Robert were asleep. His Papa fought for France – he wasn't sure just how – but he knew that Papa was more than an ordinary farmer. And he was so proud. He couldn't, of course, breathe a word to anyone – well, no one but his two best friends, Jean and Yves – and he'd tell them as soon as he was sure it would be safe to do so.

Even now, his *Maman* and Papa didn't know he had found the girl the evening before. They had tried to keep her a secret, but he had heard her breathing in the barn when he put his bicycle away. He thought at first it was the cow but she was still in the barnyard. The girl had been so frightened. Her brown eyes, round like saucers, filled with tears when he walked around the stall and saw her curled up in the horse blanket on the clean straw. A first she didn't speak but stared at him as if he carried a machine gun instead of the tire pump for his soft front tire. She looked at him and he looked at her, and then he simply pumped up his front tire and let her get used to his being there.

Finally, though, his curiosity got the best of him and he asked, "Who are you and why are you in my barn?"

She thought a moment and replied, "I am Annaliesa and I am here because a man brought me and told me to stay here. Is this your barn?"

"Well, it is the barn of my family. Where's your family?"

Bad question. He shouldn't have asked. She began to weep, to sob.

Snuffling but finally with a bit of control, she said, "We came from Liège - in Belgium. Now they, Mama and Papa, are working in Germany, I think, though I don't know where. They got on a train with the German soldiers in Siorac. Papa put me in a trunk and then the man, a priest, opened it and gave me some soup and I slept. I was there for a couple of days. Then he brought me here in the dark I have been so frightened and so cold. The woman here is nice, and she gave me clothes and some food, and the man gave me this blanket. They are going to take me to Spain where they say I will be safe." She finally took a breath. "But I am not sure I want to go to Spain. I don't know how I will ever find my Mama and Papa. They won't know to look for me in Spain…"

She took another breath and Thierry jumped in. "She is my *Maman* – the woman. When will you go…to Spain, I mean?"

"I don't know. They say 'tonight' each day….Do you know where the church is?"

"Of course I know where the church is. My best friend's father is the *sacristain* there," Thierry said, almost bursting with importance.

"What is a *sacristain*?"

"What do you mean? It is the person who takes care of the church! Don't you know anything?" Thierry said, a bit too indignantly.

"I am pretty sure there is no *sacristain* in a synagogue. I have never heard of one anyway."

"What's a sina…whatever you said?"

"I'm Jewish. We don't go to a church. The synagogue is where we go to pray and study – like a church, sort of."

"So if…well then, why do you want to go to the church?"

"I don't…want to go there, I mean. The man told me not to leave this place! I have a tiny painting that I need to sell to the church, or someone in the church if they can buy it. My Papa gave it to me in case I needed some money. It is a special picture of your Virgin Mary so it should be in a church, don't you think? It is painted by a man named Andrea di Verrochio who was a teacher of Leonardo di Vinci!"

"I could take it to the church for you." Thierry nearly crowed. He had heard of Leonardo in school.

"Could you then bring me the money from its sale? Who would buy it? Do you know someone?" She looked at him skeptically but she trusted him, something about his eyes.

"My friend's father, the *sacristain*, will know what to do with it," Thierry ventured. "I can take it in the morning when we go to Mass."

So the deal was struck. Neither of them had any idea of the worth of the little painting but Thierry thought some coins in her pocket would be useful for her journey.

That night, Thierry barely slept. He had the tiny canvas rolled into a cylinder and wrapped in a piece of brown paper he found in his mother's kitchen. He knew, of course, where he would hide it: in the handlebars of his bicycle - the perfect place! No one would look there.

All night long, lying in the dark beside his brother, he imagined what things could go wrong. Yves' papa could be angry that he knew about the girl. His own papa could find out and keep him from fulfilling his promise to Annaliesa.

He did so want to do this thing for her - to help her get to safety. He knew that the Germans hated the Jews, that they took them to bad places, that it was very bad to even know a Jew. He knew all this, but he also knew his papa was trying to help her and he wanted to be part of the effort even if he couldn't tell his papa yet. Thierry wanted to show his papa that he could be a *resistante* also and they could work together.

Dawn finally came and the two brothers, Thierry and Robert, went through the whole dreaded process of washing for mass. First their faces and then behind their ears. Why did God care about the dirt behind their ears? But *Maman* cared and that was enough.

Maman and Papa walked into the village and Robert went with them. It was Thierry's turn to ride their bicycle and he was, of course, the last to leave home. As he carefully stuffed the precious cargo, safely wrapped in the sheet of brown paper, into the handlebar and peddled into town, he felt both important and more than just a little bit scared.

When he got to the church, he haphazardly "parked" the bicycle by the fence of Yves' papa's garden next to the church and stuck his finger into the handlebar to assure himself the package was still wedged there. It was. Then he scampered into the church just barely in time to cross himself, genuflect and slither into the pew next to his brother and his parents without drawing too much attention. He leaned sideways and located first Jean and finally Yves in the pew and smiled a knowing smile at them.

Soon he could tell them what he was doing and they would be so impressed!

Linda Conn Amstutz

Chapter SIXTEEN

September 9, 1995, after the Friday Market

Langnac

Margaret

So now we know where the white van is and that Yves knows where Jean is – he won't tell us. Theoretically this should be comforting. At least his disappearance wasn't violent or his friend would not be telling us he was fine…I think.

Clare drove home silently. Had this had been a cartoon, they would have drawn smoke coming from her ears. She contained her ire until we got into the courtyard and out of the car and then…hands on hips, chest out and spitting saliva:

"The nerve of him! Telling us not to worry! Why didn't he just tell us what is really going on? Does he think we're the enemy? And the enemy of whom? For crying out loud, I am in love with the man. I wouldn't do anything to harm him! And if he were going to tell us anyway, why the hell wait until today? I have been a wreck! And you have too! That is just cruel! Damn him anyway!" Clare was stomping her feet and marching roughly in the direction of her front door, but sort of around in circles too.

I sure couldn't fault her for being angry; I was pretty angry myself. And confused. What possible reason could these two have for all the secrecy? Jean may not be in trouble, but what is he in? I need to find out and Clare needs to know too. She has learned to love and trust this guy and if he isn't lovable and trustworthy we need to know this, and we need to know why and right now it isn't looking good – especially for the trustworthy part.

As we approached the house the phone was ringing and Clare fumbled for her keys, found them and got the front door open just about the time the ringer quit.

"Oh Marg! Maybe that was him! Yves must have told him how worried we were and he called to put our minds at rest...maybe..."

She looked at me and all I could do was nod in agreement. She doesn't deserve this worry. Perhaps she was right – she would be better off alone so at least she was safe from getting her heart broken again. As I watched her face, I saw it change from the adolescent hope of a moment ago to the mature realism -- that it was probably a telemarketer.

Then the phone began to ring again.

Clare reached out and picked it up and said "Allo?"

I could see from the front door who was on the other end of the call as her face came alight and she said, "Where ARE you?" There was a pause, then, "Where have you been? Why didn't you let me know? We were so worried!" Another pause. "Yes, yes, yes, I can, we can...when? Okay, I'll be there... Jean? I love you."

I was thinking how, in a heartbeat/a phone call, Clare's world had changed – when, in fact nothing had changed at all. We still knew nothing (except that he was alive and able to talk on the telephone) but she was no longer afraid that she had lost her lover forever and she had hope of seeing him, apparently soon.

I regarded her like a dog with one ear raised. "Him?"

She smiled and looked back. "He's in Paris. He'll be on the 5:06 train in Bordeaux and he wants me to pick him up then."

"Are you NUTS? Where did he say he has been? What could he possibly have told you that would make all this OK?"

She grinned and said, "He will tell us on the way from Bordeaux. I want you to come with me. So does he."

"Are you sure he will be on this train?"

"Of course! Why wouldn't he be?"

"Well, for starters, because he took off without telling you, without his cellphone, or without even closing his door... There is something strange going on here, and you bet your life I'm going with you. No way would I let you go alone!"

"OK, we will need to leave here in about an hour and a half. I am going to make some tea, would you like some?"

"Sure, I'll be right back."

And I ran up the little pathway to "my" *pigeonnier*. I wanted to grab my written list and ask him all the questions and probably a few more. This guy wasn't getting off easily, not if I had anything to do with it.

Even if Clare wasn't thinking straight, I was!

Linda Conn Amstutz

Chapter SEVENTEEN

Margaret

Now, I am a fairly independent type of woman - certainly my parents would have, probably with chagrin, described me as such. But I completely understand Clare's about-face. I have been "in love," or thought I was, and the rational part of my brain which should lead one to a reasonable and independent conclusion seems to...cease functioning under those circumstances. Loving a man and being "in love" are not the same thing and while I wouldn't want to never have been "in love" – it feels so good and the sex is terrific – I can't recommend it for so many reasons, not the least of which is the example I have just witnessed.

This guy had a lot of explaining to do, and Clare was not going to put his explanation thru her "bullshit filter". She was just going to revel in the sound of his voice and the touch of his hand and buy whatever he says – hook, line and sinker.

I had seen that look on her face before, and on my own, and I remember what it feels like to want to believe so much that you...you just suspend your better judgement. Given enough time she would return to her normal mental acuity, I believed, I hoped. But for now, as her friend, I had to keep my wits about me and attempt at least, to point out what she should be able to see on her own but...wouldn't.

This is one thing about John that I like. We are friends, dear friends, but I have never been in that "ga ga" state where he is concerned; never had those blinders that prevent rational thought; and I can truly say that ours is a more mature man-woman relationship than I have ever experienced. I think I have a realistic expectation of where we might be going and I like that feeling. I am in possession of my faculties and I like that too. My feelings aren't crushed when he gets tied up with some parish problem and doesn't call me until the evening (when I am at home, he usually calls a couple times during the afternoon), and I don't worry that he has lost interest in me when we see each other only once or twice a week. We both have quite busy, full lives. I haven't felt as though sex would keep him with me or the lack of it drive him away. It is a pleasant addition to our already warm and satisfying relationship. I have had ga ga sex and the downside of it is just not worth the angst.

I feel content with John. I'm safe in his company. I don't want more than he is willing to give and I think he is similarly satisfied. It is almost as if we had known and been used to each other's ways for years. There is a very low level of panic in our relationship. It feels blessed, as though there were some sort of golden light shining on us when we are together.

And yet, I can't say I am comfortable with the next step. Living together isn't an option in his line of work, so the next step is a permanent one...or at least it is supposed to be – "'til death do us part".

Of course, in the U.S. over 50% of the time it doesn't work out that way. I have a feeling that he will take his time and that he will be sure I am ready before he asks "the question". It is one of those "guy" things where they have to really stick their neck out a mile and the surer they are of what the answer will be, the smaller the chance of their neck getting chopped off! So he will give me the time I need, I am reasonably confident of that. I am over fifty and at this age some women might be getting anxious – but I like where we are now and I can wait…until the next step feels as natural as the one we are in now. I just hope my being away isn't working the "absence makes the heart grow fonder" thing on John. That could throw all this "comfort" into a tailspin and mess up a good thing.

Chapter EIGHTEEN

September 9, 1995

On the road to Bordeaux

We scrambled into Clare's little blue Renault and headed down the steep drive and out onto the main road heading for Bordeaux. The trip should take about an hour - we just made it three days ago. I was not sure what to say as we headed for the train station and our meeting with Jean Bertrand.

I felt like I was walking the fence here with Clare. I didn't want to insult her intelligence or her sanity but also I was thinking that neither of those two things was working to the fullest extent of its capabilities just now. She was just so happy to know that in about an hour she would see and touch the man she had come to love, and I didn't trust him any farther than…well, not much. I wanted her to be a little bit more careful than she wants to be. I wanted her to at least ask some probing questions – or I would. I read her the list I had made and we added a couple of points.

I reminded her that he had been gone for two, almost three days now and didn't tell her a thing - not even when he finally called. I reminded her that Yves, however comforting he seemed, didn't really tell us anything either. The reason might be something dangerous, or illegal or both!

I, too was charmed by Jean Bertrand - but he had a lot of explaining to do and I was inclined, at least at first, to just be quiet and see where he took it. If he were honest and transparent, fine; if shifty and circumspect, then we needed to be ready to…what? He lived next door to Clare - it would be really awkward for her if he turned out to be a cad.

She wanted me to add asking him why he felt he couldn't tell her what was going on so she didn't worry. I explained that I was fairly sure he would address that question without our having to ask and it sounded a little on the whiney/clingy side. And I thought perhaps she'd best let him have a chance to take the initiative on this subject. I was very willing to either let him be a hero and address it on his own or else let him dig the hole miles deeper by NOT telling her – and maybe she would see the light. If indeed there was a light to see. For all I knew he would have rational explanations for all that has happened…whatever that might be. I didn't believe him to be a villain necessarily; I just didn't know.

We wanted to ask, of course, where he had been, and why he left in such a rush and what Yves had to do with this. And why Yves knew (and Clare didn't) just what had been going on. Perhaps we should even ask if all this was a dangerous situation…or just…or just… what?

The drive was going fairly quickly. Of course Clare was driving 110 - but that was kilometers per hour not miles. So it was only about 60, but on these narrow winding roads it felt quite sufficiently fast. Clare had made this trip a hundred or maybe more times and she knew all the twists and turns, but we weren't late. We had time to get there before his train arrived, and the *TGV* wouldn't be early – late maybe, but never early.

"Clare, let's not come upon a farm cart around the next bend and get in a mess that makes us miss meeting his train, huh?" I suggested, trying to sound reasonable and not appear as nervous as I was. She glanced in my direction and slowed our progress some, maybe seeing reason, maybe patronizing me. Our conversation seemed to stagnate; there wasn't much to say until we learned where he had been and what he'd been doing.

There seemed to be a hundred stoplights between the edge of Bordeaux and the *Gare* Saint Jean where the fast train from Paris would arrive, but finally we were there. We parked the car and went in to check the big electronic board that tells the arrival and departure times and the tracks where each train will be. His train was due to be on track #4 and we had to walk down and then back up some steps (under tracks #1, 2 and 3) to get there. We didn't know what car he would be riding in so the best thing to do would be to stand at the beginning of the quai and wait there so he would have to walk past us. We didn't want to miss him when we are this close.

The digital clock overhead clicked from 5:05 to 5:06 and, sure enough, around the curve at the end of the station came the aerodynamic blue and silver nose of the *TGV* from Paris, right on time.

Linda Conn Amstutz

Chapter NINETEEN

Early Spring 1941 – Sunday morning

Langnac, Eglise du Notre Dame

As his parents and their friends visited on the steps and in the paved courtyard in front of the church, Thierry slipped away from Jean and Yves and followed Yves' papa out the door. He caught up with him behind the church as he went about his duties.

"M. Menton! M. Menton! Please wait a moment."

Yves' papa paused and turned around. Suddenly Thierry didn't know what to say, where to begin. He stuttered a couple of times, but his friend's father smiled and kindly said, "What is it? Tell me so I can get on with my work!"

Thierry, unable to think of anything else, said simply, "There is a girl in my barn…"

"Shush!" said M. Menton, instantly leery. "Come with me into my house. Say nothing more here!"

He put his arm around Thierry and herded him as they hurried the last few steps past the garden and into his house.

"Now, tell me how you know of this girl? You say you think she is in your barn?"

"Yes, didn't you know about her? Papa and *Maman* have been giving her food and talking of taking her to Spain! I saw her when I went in with my bicycle…and she has this picture of the holy Virgin. She needs some money and her papa told her to sell the painting if she did, so I brought it to you because I know you, and I am afraid, a little, of Père Auguste and… Well, can you help us?"

"Did your papa and *maman* tell you about this child?" M. Menton asked cautiously.

"No, I found her. I have told no one, not even Papa and *Maman*, that I spoke with her. I wanted to help so I brought this tiny painting of the Virgin to you. She –"

Annaliesa – says a teacher of Leonardo...someone painted it and it is valuable. Who would buy it? Can I get her some money for her journey? Will you help me to do this?"

Nervously, Thierry unrolled the little painting and handed it to M. Menton who carefully looked it over and smiled at him.

* * * *

Louis Menton was the *sacristain*, not a highly educated man, but he recognized that this tiny painting could have some significant value and he knew just the person to assess that value and perhaps even to buy it. He said he would take it to the owner of the chateau - the *Signeur*, M.de Rastignac – and if he hurried, he might even catch him before he left the church!

"Wait here, Thierry. I will come right back."

Louis loped out the door and across the garden to the churchyard. He looked at the parishioners departing in all directions for their homes and did not see M.

Rastignac, the Lord du Chapt de Rastignac, the owner of the Chateau de la Meynerdie just across the river, and the richest of all the parishioners. Surely he would help by buying the small painting but where had he gone?

Time was short, and this could not take too long. Some choices are simply not ones for which one has preparation. They have not answers of black and white. One has to rely on the feeling of right and the feeling of wrong and simply do the best one can.

Louis did something he had never even thought of doing before. He went back into the church and took several bills from the collection plates. It felt like the right thing to do. He hid the painting in a niche inside the hollowed wall behind the altar and hurried back to his house where the boy waited

---

* * * *

To Thierry it seemed forever before M. Menton returned but when he did, in his hand he held a wad of currency which he handed to him. "Give this to the girl. It probably isn't enough but it will help her on her journey. Hurry now; your family is ready to leave and I saw Yves and Jean in the churchyard waiting for you. You must tell no one about this...not even Yves and Jean. Promise me this now! It could mean serious trouble. You must promise me right now. I will know if you say anything."

"I'll tell no one." Thierry said, he took the bills with shaking fingers, but he wasn't sure what "serious trouble" M. Menton meant or how he might know, and he wanted so much to share this amazing secret with Jean and Yves.

Still, he promised.

Then he carefully rolled the bills tightly into a cylindrical shape, wrapped the piece of brown paper which had enclosed the painting around the notes and slipped them into his sleeve. He looked at M. Menton's serious face once more, turned and left the house. Now he was going to have to see his best friends and not share the secret which was already trying to burst from his lips.

Thierry saw the German soldier first as he came around the corner of the house. The tall man glanced at the crowd but, so far, had no reason to pay any attention to the villagers and farmers. Thierry affected an air of indifference to the world and sauntered directly to his friends, then quietly said to them, "Come with me. I can't tell you why just yet, but just do as I ask."

Chapter TWENTY

Sunday morning, Spring 1941,

Outside the village of Langnac

Winded and feeling as if his legs were made of rubber like the tires of his bicycle, Thierry dismounted, looked all around and walked into the barn, pushing the squeaking rusty bicycle ahead of him. He rested it against the wall just to the left of the sliding door. Slipping the cylindrical brown paper-wrapped roll of money out of the handlebar and gripping it tightly, he wrestled the heavy door closed behind himself. No one would be able to surprise them without opening the noisy barn door first.

"Annaliesa? Are you here? It is I, Thierry. I have some money for you," Thierry whispered as he peered around the edge of the stall where she had been just last evening. He saw nothing.

She was gone!

He looked in the other stall and then glanced up just in time to see her dark head disappear behind a bale of hay. He climbed the ladder and quietly called to her again this time she responded. "I was so frightened! I heard the Germans go by on the road in their truck and everyone was gone, so I came up here to hide. I was sure they were coming for me." Her voice shook. "Then the barn door opened and I couldn't really see clearly who it was. I am so very happy it was you!" And she reached out and hugged him.

Now Thierry had never been hugged by a girl, except, of course, his *maman*. Embarrassed, he shrugged her away.

"Here." He proudly shoved his fist and the money in her direction. "Yves' papa says it isn't enough but it will help you on your journey. I have told no one of this - not even my best friends!"

"Thank you, Thierry. I am very grateful." She put her hands on his shoulders and softly kissed his left cheek. The blood rushed to his face and he could feel the damp place where her lips had been.

He scrambled crab-like backwards and nearly fell down the ladder from the hayloft. Then turning and almost banging into the big door, he slid it open just wide enough to get through, and met his parents and brother walking through the courtyard toward the house. Stammering a greeting, he went into the house and up to the room he shared with his brother, wiping the place on his cheek where her kiss had been with the back of his hand.

Shortly afterwards, Thierry heard his papa climb the stairs to his room. He entered without announcement.

"M. Menton told me what you have been doing, Thierry. Look at me. I want you to understand how very dangerous this is. I want you to stop, NOW! This is enough. You have helped the girl and I thank you for that but it must stop. Do you understand? And you must tell no one."

His voice was quiet and held a tremor Thierry had not heard before. He looked up into his papa's eyes and saw something he didn't recognize. Was his papa afraid? He'd wanted to help, thought his papa would be proud of him, treat him like an equal in the great fight for France. What was this? He didn't understand.

"Papa, I have told no one, not even Yves and Jean. I was careful; I trusted only M. Menton as I know you do. I want to help you. I see you go out into the night and I know you must be fighting for France. I, too am French and I want to help."

"Oh, Thierry," his papa said, enfolding him in his strong arms and trembling at the same time, "I know you do, but there is so much you do not know, so much you cannot yet understand. There is so much danger.

"I do not fight, Thierry, I only try to help those escaping the German persecution. I try to save lives, not to take them. You, my son, must not endanger yourself in this way because, should something happen to me, you and Robert will need to help your mother. You are the oldest and she will need you. You must remain safe. Do you understand? No more of this nonsense? Will you promise me?"

Of course Thierry wanted to promise, but could he? He so wanted to help and he had been so careful Nothing would happen to him. He could not reply. He just stayed in his papa's embrace and listened to his heart beat and to his quiet breathing and felt safe in the warmth of his papa's love.

"Now, find your brother, go out to the field by the road and begin the planting of the maize. I must do an errand in Challerville and I will help you when I return, but the planting cannot wait."

And his father was gone on the bicycle, as Thierry could hear the squeaking and whining into the distance.

He decided the excitement for the day was over and he corralled Robert, and they began the tedious job of planting the maize seeds by hand - in rows as even as two boys of their tender age could make them.

The afternoon dragged on row after row. The boys worked together to begin again the cycle of growth that has formed this community for hundreds of years.

War or no war, the crops were planted and the harvest would come…they hoped.

Chapter TWENTY-ONE

Sunday morning, Spring 1941

Outside the village of Langnac

Sandrine

Sandrine glanced out the door to see what progress her sons had made in the planting of the maize and noted their statue-like stillness. By what were they so captivated? She watched for a bit and then walked out the kitchen door and saw her friends Sylvie and Arnauld pushing a bicycle down the road, turning up her lane, looking for her. Roland had taken their bicycle. Where was Roland?

The Bertrands lived in the village and while it wasn't far, only a couple of kilometres, a Sunday afternoon visit was unusual. And where was their son Jean?

Sandrine could feel the hair stand up on the back of her neck, the blood drain from her face, and her knees weaken.

Where was Roland?

He had taken their bicycle to Challerville. It was a noisy bicycle they were pushing but there certainly was no shortage of dilapidated machinery in France these days. - as the Germans had taken everything that worked! Perhaps it wasn't their bicycle after all.

Three more rows and the boys would come into the courtyard for their rest break and a drink of water from the well. Planting was thirsty work in the warm spring sunshine.

So where was Roland?

She slowly walked to the door opening onto the courtyard as the Bertrands came through the gate. She looked at them, saw the expressions, or rather the lack of expression, on their faces and she sat on the step -

sat as her legs had turned to jelly. She knew this visit was not for a friendly Sunday afternoon chat.

She felt the fear and then the tears formed in her eyes. No words were spoken as she recognized for sure the bicycle Arnauld was propping against the wall, then Sylvie sat beside her on one side, Arnauld on the other and they held her in their arms as her sobs began.

First there were tears, and her body shook but no sound came from Sandrine. Her grief was too deep for sound. Her life was over - at least the life she wanted to live. From here on it would be one without her life-long partner. She had only her boys. They sat there for...how long? No one knew, but eventually the boys walked in from the field for their water break, and she knew she had to ...had to what? What was there to do now?

"*Maman?*" said Thierry "What...?"

Sandrine was thankful as Arnauld answered for her.

"Boys, come here." Then softly he said, "Your father has been killed and you must now help your *maman* to be strong. Be with her, she needs you."

And the boys, not in the least comprehending how completely this would change their lives, went and let their *maman* hold them close to her. Sandrine trembled as did they as thoughts of their lives without husband and papa flicked through their minds.

"Sandrine, I am sorry to be so abrupt, but I must go. Roland's body is at the edge of the wood and it must be buried before the Bosch find it - if indeed they did not put it there in the first place. We do not know who did this and he did not have the papers for the girl; at least when I found him he did not." Arnauld stood up.

"No! You will not bury my husband! No!" Sandrine said with a vehemence she didn't know she possessed.

"But I must, and it needs to be soon. Best that you say he simply left and did not come back - you know nothing, he is just 'gone'. Do you understand?"

"Yes, I understand, but I will go with you. I am grateful for your help but I must do this. It is not for you to do. He was my husband and I will do this."

Sandrine's voice quavered but she stood firm and Arnauld, (with a spade fetched from the barn by Robert), took her hand in his other and, as Sylvie stayed with the boys, they walked out of the courtyard and toward the wood and Roland's rapidly cooling corpse.

While Sandrine wasn't sure she wanted to know the answers to them, she was sure her boys would be full of questions and so as they walked she asked Arnaud:

"How was Roland killed?"

"By a gun"

"Where? "

"By the edge of the *forêt* de Double near the Challerville road."

"By whom?"

"No one knows"

"Did he have the papers for the girl?"

"He may have had, but he didn't when he was found"

"What will happen to the girl now?"

"She will be moved tonight; I will arrange with Roland's brother to do this."

And then they were there. With difficulty, both physical and emotional, Sandrine and Arnauld carried Roland's body to a spot deep in the wood, almost completely surrounded by brambles, as secret a spot as they could find. With luck no one else would discover it and the story about his simply disappearing might work.

It seemed to Sandrine to take no time for Arnauld to dig the trench deep enough that the forest animals would not disinter Roland's body, which was no longer bleeding from the single bullet hole in his chest.

Sandrine knelt beside him, picked up his still warm hand and tried to pray, but she couldn't think, couldn't talk with the God who had allowed this to happen. She just sat and held the hand she would never hold again after this day, and quietly she wept.

The two of them lifted his body and nestled it into the grave, but when Arnauld picked up the shovel to cover his body with dirt, Sandrine firmly took hold of his arm. She looked at him with eyes full of a grief he could not deny and said, "No!"

She took the spade from his hands. "This is for me to do." Then she slowly, tears running down her cheeks, shovelled the soft just-dug soil over her beloved husband's cooling body. At that moment she remembered her boys and ceased wishing she, too, were lying in the ground.

When she had finished, they placed some flat rocks on top of the disturbed earth and covered them with dead leaves and forest clutter. It was the best they could do for him.

Sandrine would remember the place and he would have a proper marker and some proper prayers. Someday. Someday after this war.

His arm around her shoulder, Arnauld led her from the wood, and he told her that he must get back to town as his absence must not be noticed and Jean was at home by himself.

Sylvie could stay with her for a while but she must be home by dark. The curfew.

Then he asked the unthinkable. "Could one of the boys take a message to Roland's brother, Pierre, about the girl? She must be moved and it has to be very soon. Tonight."

She stared at him, unbelieving. Was she, now, meant to risk her boys' lives?

"What?"

He told her that Thierry already understood about the girl and as he was the oldest he probably was the right one. If he rode his bicycle, he could get there before dark and then stay with his Tante Marie.

How had Arnauld worked all this out? Sandrine could barely put one foot before the other. How could she let Thierry go? She'd lost Roland. Could she chance losing Thierry too? No!

But then, there was the girl. Arnauld was right. She'd been there much too long already. If the Germans found her they would all be killed. Thierry had ridden to his uncle's many times. It would look less suspicious for the boy to go than anyone else.

Numbly, she looked at Arnaud and silently nodded her ascent.

Sandrine finally prayed.

Chapter TWENTY-TWO

Sunday afternoon, spring 1941

The road to Bergerac

Papa was dead.

Thierry tried to see the curving road through the tears that kept wanting to come to his eyes. He couldn't cry; he had to see where he was going and do the job he'd been given. His papa had told him that there was so much he didn't know about the danger. Surely he knew now. He tried to think what it really meant that Papa was dead, killed, never ever coming home. He just couldn't make thoughts of the future come to his mind that didn't have Papa in them. No matter how hard he tried to think of the harvest, his next birthday, even going to church next week - Papa was there in his imagination. He pedalled hard but the exertion didn't bring him the peace it usually did.

Thierry remembered the times he had ridden to his *Oncle* Pierre's farm in the past, quiet times, riding through the rolling hills and along the river. He had never been in a hurry to get there like he was today. Too much of the day had gone before he had begun. He pushed hard and harder, and slowly the peace began to fill in.

Maman had been so brave. She had gone with M. Bertrand into the woods to bury his father, then when they had returned *Madame* Bertrand had taken her up to her bed to rest. M. Bertrand had told him that he - HE, Thierry, was now the man of the house and he must do this thing - he must get to his uncle and tell him the awful news. He must ask *Oncle* Pierre to fetch the girl, Annaliesa, and take her without papers to Spain. Would *Oncle* Pierre listen to him? It had always been a fun trip to Bergerac - but this was not fun.

He could feel the fear running up the back of his spine and the hair on the back of his neck tingled. This was grown up and serious and really scary. This was what his father had been talking about, and he was right, he wasn't ready. Would he get there before dark? He had never been stopped by the Germans before… but this was different - always before he had been mostly innocent. This time he was on a mission and it was deadly serious. Deadly.

"I am the oldest" he thought. "I must take care of *Maman* and Robert. I must do the things that Papa did." But how? I don't KNOW how to do those things.

"You must remain safe." his papa had said. "you need to help your mother - the oldest…she will need you…Promise me?" but he hadn't promised. He withheld the oath his papa had asked for. And here he was, riding for all he was worth through the early evening toward Bergerac and his uncle's farm. He had wished earlier that he had given his promise - it was what his papa had wanted, but now he was glad he had not. He was doing just what his papa had been afraid of - carrying a message telling his uncle to fetch the girl, and take her to safety. Safety? She might be going to safety but Thierry wondered if he would ever be safe ...like he had felt that very afternoon with his papa's strong arms around him.

The low lying areas of the rolling hills were woven with wisps of fog as the sun slipped lower and lower in the western sky. He was getting close, soon he would be at his uncle's farm. To the east there was already a big moon - was it rising or setting? He thought it might be better for their journey toward Spain if it were setting and the night would be lit only by the stars.

Jerked from his thoughts, Thierry heard an engine - in the distance but getting closer. It was coming toward him, not from behind, but from Bergerac. There were many Germans in Bergerac. His heart began to race in his chest and he rode faster and faster. He'd ridden, waving at the soldiers who, by now, were familiar with the laughing boy from the farm near Siorac, right through the check-point near his home. He then thought he was home free. Now the motor droned closer and closer. Over the rise in the distance he saw one headlight - a German on a motorcycle! He rode faster and pasted a smile on his face, waving with one hand as the German passed. The soldier slowed and looked back over his shoulder and then turned toward the front and kept going. Thierry heaved a huge sigh of relief and kept on over the hill and shortly afterward turned into the lane that would take him to the farm of his uncle.

Tante Marie was in the *potager* (kitchen garden) and saw him coming up the lane and she called to her husband who walked from the orchard so that they stood together as Thierry breathlessly related the devastating events of the day. His *Tante* Marie, childless herself, enveloped him in her ample arms and held him to her bosom as the comfort of her embrace finally loosened the tears Thierry had been so valiantly holding back. By the time his tears had been dried, his *Oncle* Pierre had already taken his bicycle and gone to get the girl. Thierry was safe for the time being but he now knew too much of these grown up things to ever feel the confidence of a child again.

Tante Marie was usually Thierry's biggest supporter - when he and his mother disagreed, *Tante* Marie seemed not to be on *Maman's* side exactly as you might expect a grown up to be - rather she took Thierry aside and explained, reasoned and sometimes quietly agreed with Thierry all the while encouraging him to do whatever his *maman* wanted..."just this once." Thierry knew he was *Tante* Marie's favorite without anyone having said it. This evening however there was no changing her mind. Thierry wanted to go home and his dear aunt was not going to allow it to happen. It was dark now and *Oncle* Pierre had taken the bicycle and that was the end of the discussion. Thierry would stay there, have some supper and then perhaps a steaming mug of the chocolate *Tante* Marie had hidden away for just such an emergency.

A pot of something smelling marvellous bubbled on *Tante* Marie's stove and she had some real bread! Perhaps it wouldn't be so bad staying here tonight after all. *Tante* Marie , gesturing to the small square basket beside the stove asked Thierry "Bring some wood for the stove from the woodshed" (just outside the kitchen door) and he hurried to do it, eager to please his aunt, and still full of nervous energy in spite of the planting and the long ride to her farm.

It was full dark now and the moon, which had indeed been rising, was now above the trees and was so bright it made distinct shadows in the barnyard. Thierry wondered if his papa's spirit was looking down from heaven on him and if he were proud of him for bringing the news to his aunt and uncle. He wondered if he should talk to his papa - would he be heard?

"Papa, I am sorry I couldn't promise to stop helping France. I am sorry if you are disappointed in me. Please understand that I had to ride to *Oncle* Pierre and tell him to come and get Annaliesa. I am responsible now for this and also for *Maman*. Don't be angry with me, Papa. I miss you and I love you…

"Amen" he added as an afterthought…

"Thierry! To whom are you talking? Hurry back inside and bring the wood!" *Tante* Marie rasped from the kitchen doorway. She seemed upset.

"I was trying to talk to my papa in heaven, to ask him not to be angry with me for helping France by coming here and bringing the message to *Oncle* Pierre - just this morning he asked me to promise to stay safe and that if anything were to happen to him I had to care for *Maman* and I, I...I couldn't promise, I didn't promise him. And now he is dead and I am here and..." and Thierry began to cry again as *Tante* Marie clasped him to her once more. "My poor, poor child, I am sure your papa is proud of you and your *maman* will be fine for this night. You did what you had to do and we are all grateful for that. You are safe and I am sure your papa knows this."

"How will *Oncle* Pierre get Annaliesa to Spain? Is it far? I don't know even which way they would go. Are there horses? Will they ride? Tell me *Tante*! Are there Germans there? When will he be home...*Oncle* Pierre?"

"So many questions! Well, Thierry, they will walk and it is a very long way but *Oncle* Pierre goes only part of the way - only to the foothills of the mountains then the girl will go with others the rest of the way over the mountains and into Catalonia. Catalonia is a part of Spain. It will be a very hard journey for her but the men will protect her. Please don't worry. *Oncle*

Picrre will be home sometime tomorrow, perhaps. Maybe the next day. Now, eat your soup and I have a treat for you when you have done that. Please don't worry - *Oncle* Pierre has taken many people on this journey and he knows the way well."

She sat him down on the bench by the scrubbed pine table in the big country kitchen and before him was a bowl of vegetable soup and a large slice of bread and some watered wine for him to help him to sleep. He ate, realizing suddenly how hungry he was, and drank and then the magical steaming chocolate appeared and that was the last Thierry remembered before waking in *Tante* Marie's bed the next morning.

It was to be his first morning without his papa.

Linda Conn Amstutz

Chapter TWENTY-THREE

September 9th 1995

Gare Saint Jean, Bordeaux

There were hoards of people getting off this train from Paris and it seemed every one of them was in a hurry. Clare and I had to flatten ourselves against a pillar from time to time to keep from having our toes run over by a rolling valise or a porter's cart. At last she saw him!

To her credit, Clare waited for him to get to the place where we stood. Jean wrapped her in his arms and she wept.

"I am so sorry, Clare," he said, "I really did have to leave so abruptly and yes, I want to tell you - to tell both of you, all about it. Do we need to go to Langnac in a hurry, or is there time for a restorative glass of wine at the cafe across the street from the station?"

I answered that question.

I certainly did NOT want Clare simultaneously trying to drive and listen to this tale!

"Yes!" I said emphatically, "We do have time, and that's a welcome suggestion!"

So we walked across the street and found a table under some pollarded plane trees just beginning to turn the golden rust signifying the end of summer and ordered a bottle of the crisp white wine of Bordeaux. It came quickly, in a battered aluminum bucket of water and a little ice, and Jean poured out a glass for each of us before sharing his astounding story.

"I am so very sorry for having worried you, ma *chérie*. I left in such a rush, I didn't even take my phone! Thierry came and he was afraid, no, he was sure that someone was following him and we had to go *maintenant*! (NOW!) I am not even certain I closed the door. We left so fast and then Thierry drove like a madman, and I had no idea what was happening. We took the little lane which passes through the forest and the bottom of his little van kept bumping on the rutted road! It wasn't until we arrived at La Garde and got on the departmental road toward Langnac that he began to explain. *Mon Dieu*! What a story he told me!"

He took a few sips of his wine as we were listening attentively. He had yet to reveal the reason for his urgent departure.

Jean continued. "It seems that Yves had phoned Thierry earlier and told him that the American artisans who were installing the new organ in the church had found an empty space in a wall which had previously been thought to be solid. They had to change the position of the largest pipes for the organ because of the reverberation from the hollowness of the wall. Yves had not known it was hollow - at least in that place he had not.

"Before the workers arrived on Thursday Yves was inspecting the section of wall that had been broken through and saw something stuck into a cleft within the hollow and reached in and brought it out. It was a very small piece of canvas rolled loosely in brown paper - a painting. It was very beautiful. He knew, of course, what it was but simply couldn't believe his eyes. For fifty years he had thought this painting was in the hands of M. de Rastignac but Yves had never seen the painting himself. He tried to think what to do and the only thing he could think of was to call Thierry. Thierry, you see, was the only one of the three of us who had actually seen the painting."

Clare stopped him at this point. "What painting? What are you talking about, Jean? I am afraid I am lost."

"Good for you, Clare, keep his feet to the fire!" I thought to myself.

"Ah, ma *chérie*, I am sorry. It is a miniature painting of the Madonna, the Mother of Christ - painted in the middle ages by Andrea del Verrocchio, a teacher of Leonardo da Vinci – and it belonged to a young Jewish girl back in the war we spoke of at dinner the other night. It was in the spring of 1941 and she was hiding from the Germans in Thierry's family's barn.

Thierry's papa was trying to help her to get safely out of France. She needed money for her journey and she wanted to sell...not really sell...trade the painting for some money to help her on her journey. She gave the painting to Thierry..."

"A child?" Clare and I, looking at each other, exclaimed together.

"She gave a masterpiece like that to a little boy?" Clare continued.

"You must understand, ladies, it was very different then. She was desperate, she needed funds and the painting was all she had. Her father, who had been an art dealer in Liège in Belgium had given it to her for just this purpose. He told her to do this when she needed money. She gave it to Thierry because Thierry told her he knew the sacristain of the church, and it was, after all a picture of the Virgin. So Thierry took it to the person he thought most likely to know what to do with it. Yves' papa was then the sacristain of the church just as Yves is today. Yves and I were there when Thierry made this exchange, though we did not know exactly what he was doing. It was not until much later that Thierry was able to tell Yves and me about the details, after his papa was killed and after he came back from his Tante Marie's farm in Bergerac.

"Yves' papa gave Thierry some money, and he then gave it to the girl. Thierry always thought the money must have come from M. de Rastignac, the chateau owner. That was the last we knew of any of this until Yves found the tiny painting in the crevice inside the hollow wall. He phoned Thierry to come and be certain that it was indeed the same painting - how could it be otherwise? But Yves wanted to be sure.

"When Thierry arrived, one of the workers – not the American artisans who were installing the organ, but one of the Russian laborers tearing out the wall – overheard Yves and Thierry and came into his house and tried to take the painting from them. He clearly was a thug and thought he could steal it and make some money quickly. He threatened them and the two of them somehow got away. They took both Yves car and Thierry's van and drove in two different directions. Yves got the Russian to follow him and Thierry came to my house to get me."

I interrupted, "Why you? What did they want you to do?"

"Ah, Margaret, I lived for many years in Paris and I have a very dear friend there who is a dealer in art. We hoped Michel could assure us as to the authenticity of the painting and perhaps even estimate its worth. He might even know of its provenance and it would be a start to finding the proper owner.

"We – Thierry and I - drove to Bordeaux. Thierry dropped me here at the train station and I took the painting on the train to Paris.

"Such works, Michel tells me, are difficult to authenticate with certainty, but the painter, Andrea del Verrocchio, who, in the early Renaissance, was also a goldsmith and a sculptor, was a master painter in the court of Lorenzo and Giuliano de Medici and taught the young Leonardo, Pietro Perugino, Lorenzo de Credi and Botticelli. Often the early works of the pupils are difficult to distinguish from those of the teacher, so much do they try to imitate his style and techniques.

"Michel and his friends at the Louvre went through an exhaustive process to verify that this painting was what we all thought…well, all that we were told it was. And it seems that indeed it is!

"The authentication process is painstaking and both subjective and very scientific. They can do a digital statistical analysis of the various layers in a work and the brush or pen strokes of an artist then compare another work with the same statistical information. Also there are a couple of machines that perform spectrophotometric analyses to tell if there is an element in the paint that was not typical of the age in which it was supposed to have been painted - all very interesting and certainly over my head…

"I left it with him as it may indeed be much more valuable than we imagined and he has the facilities for safekeeping that such a piece requires. Michel has no client at present who would buy such a work. He thinks it should be sold at auction, that is if we cannot find the girl…woman, first.

"Its worth is likely in the tens of millions of Francs," Jean said, and by now, Clare and I both wondered many things.

Clare looked for a long time at Jean, who took an-other sip of his wine, cocked her head to the side and asked him, as though she was not sure she wanted to hear the answer, "So, Jean, to whom does this precious little work of art belong now?"

Jean looked back just as thoughtfully. "I have spoken with M. de Rastignac and he knows nothing of it - has never seen it. Perhaps his father did, but his father died several years ago. I don't know where the money came from, so I think the painting might belong to the girl - a woman, an old woman now…if we had any idea how to find her or even if she still lives. I suppose an argument could be made that it belongs to the church since it has been there this very long time and the fact that we really don't know where the money came from that M. Menton gave Thierry, but really the girl got such a pittance for it when she left for Spain. Clare, I really don't know."

"How ever in the world could someone find her? Your father is gone, Yves' father is no longer living and Thierry's died during the war. Who would even know where she went?" Clare posed.

"Yves' papa kept records for the church back then, but I don't imagine for a moment that he would include this information if he even knew where she ended up. I will have to ask Yves if he has read his papa's journals for that time. He may have since all this began last week. The girl, her given name was Annaliesa, but I don't think anyone ever knew her family name. Perhaps there are records about the provenance of the painting kept in Liège in the days before the war began. Her father's name might be in those. I think Michel could make some inquiries along those lines. If she survived the trip into Spain she may have married and then knowing her family name before the war still wouldn't help us. It is unlikely we should ever find her…very unlikely…but I think we should try."

Clare and Jean sat quietly at the little table of the *café* across from the train station in Bordeaux. Their fingers touched atop the little wooden table. They sat, together again, and I thought at that moment that this experience in the short span of a few days had taught the two of them something very important about their relationship. I didn't think they would spend much time apart in the future - it appeared to have been as hard on Jean as I know it has been on Clare, and they both knew this. I could see it and so, obviously, did they.

Jean soon looked at me as though he had just re-membered I was there. "Margaret, I am very happy that you have been here to be a friend to Clare just now; thank you."

I didn't know how to reply to that...so I didn't. I smiled. And I believed him and his story.

Jean looked at both of us in turn and said, "You know, this fellow who chased Thierry and me, and who threatened Yves, is around somewhere, and while he has no accurate idea what this painting is worth, he has got the scent of fast money that he has not had to work for. He may have friends as well. This is why I was so pleased to leave the painting with Michel - and I am pretty certain the Russian would never find Michel's identity, but I am not at all confident that we are safe as long as this fellow thinks he can profit from the situation. I don't know what sort of contacts he has and I am worried about him. I don't think, since he fol-lowed Yves on Thursday, that he knows about me or where I live - or about Thierry's name or location. Yves, however is going to be his target, his connection for the easy money."

Then I told Jean that Clare and I had gone to the *gendarmes* about his disappearance and that we had made a missing person report. I suggested it might be a good idea to enlist their help when we got back to Langnac. He would probably have to do some explaining to them since the report was now official.

Clare ventured somewhat defensively, "I was so worried about you, dear Jean, I thought they could help find you. It was only later that Yves told me that he knew where you were and that you were OK. I am sorry if it causes you problems but I would do it again in a heartbeat if I thought it would help get you back to me safely."

He leaned forward and kissed her cheek. "It is fine, Clare, I will talk with them and perhaps they can be helpful with the Russian. I am so very sorry to have worried you."

We had finished the bottle of wine and now, also, the discussion - at least for the present - so Jean paid the check, so we walked across the street once more to the parking lot and retrieved Clare's little blue Renault. We headed back to Langnac as the sun was setting behind us, driving in companionable silence after this eventful day. Soon the even breathing of Jean in the back seat turned to snores as his fatigue overcame him.

Linda Conn Amstutz

Chapter TWENTY-FOUR

Spring 1941

Near Bergerac, the farm of Thierry's *Tante* Marie and *Oncle* Pierre

Marie let the child sleep. She loved him as much as if he were her own baby - she always had. She'd helped her sister-in-law at his birth and afterward, so she knew him well. Robert was her nephew also but Thierry held a special place in her heart. And her heart was breaking for him as he had now lost his papa.

She had heard him talking last night and was terrified the Germans had followed him - it was a relief to find he'd been talking to his dead papa in heaven. A relief and a heartbreak at once. Marie had taken her final bit of chocolate to make his drink last night and she was so glad she'd kept it for this "special occasion." What else could she do to ease his pain and make his future seem brighter. Life was going to be hard for her sister-in-law, the widow Sandrine Duranthon - would have been hard even if there weren't a war but now...

Where was Pierre? It was nearly noon and usually he had returned by now when he escorted one of his "little pigeons" to his friends in the South. They had been coming more frequently, these needy little birds. British and American flyers, downed in occupied territory, some hurt, some simply frightened. French Jews, Belgian Jews, German Jews - other *Maquisards* who had been discovered by the enemy and had to disappear - all sorts of "little pigeons" as Pierre would say, "flying home to roost."

They "roosted" as short a time as was practical. Overnight, a few days...then on to a safe life in Spain or through Spain and back to the fighting, or just to somewhere it was secure enough to send a radio message to London, then back into the fray. Marie wondered if it were worth the threat to the life of her husband - all these birds.

Pierre, where was he?

To keep herself from going mad with waiting, she took her secateurs and went into the apricot orchard to trim the odd sucker and snip a branch that wandered off the proper direction, one at a time; trying to think only of the nascent blooms, fragrant and white, that would become fat, sweet, orange fruit early next summer.

She had wanted to, as a few of her neighbors had, try a small vineyard on the fallow piece of land just to the east of the apricot orchard - it ran down a hillside as it faced the rising sun, was well drained enough and had a chalky, rocky soil - good for growing the red wine grapes that had for centuries been cultivated just a bit further to the West in the Bordeaux region. Pierre said he would prefer to stay with what he knew and what his father had grown on this land which had been in his family for at least four generations that they knew of. So Marie trimmed the apricots and later she would move on to the peaches and then the apples.

She walked back toward the house, to check on Thierry who should be awake soon and was certain to be hungry as only a boy his age could be.

Thierry sat on the front step talking with someone who was standing behind the well. Was it Pierre?

She hurried her steps with relief and then she saw the man. A stranger to her - not a German, thank God! As she got closer, now near enough to hear their voices and to hear that they had stopped at her approach. She froze in her tracks. This stranger had not brought good news and instantly she did NOT want to hear his message.

Still as a marble statue and just as cold, she couldn't make her legs move, couldn't speak. She'd felt such sympathy for Sandrine just last evening; she had known this could happen to her, but now? So soon? Wasn't one death enough for this family in so short a time? No tears came and no one said a word.

The stranger moved slowly toward Marie, and she raised her hands flat open before her to stop him. Now not positive, perhaps grasping the last scrap of hope, she asked, "Is it Pierre? Is he hurt?"

The man shook his head, his eyes gave her the truth, and she felt her legs give way. He was there - catching her before she fell.

"I am sorry, Mme Duranthon." He carried her, un-speaking, into the house and Thierry followed. The boy, grown overnight beyond his years, went to the pump and got her a cup of water, handing it to her carefully making sure she could hold it without drop-ping it.

And then the man repeated, "I am so very sorry, madame. It was very sudden. They came from nowhere. He had just turned her over to me when the bullet went through his head. He felt no pain, to be sure. The child is safe. I took her to the next transfer and then went back to him. I buried his body this morning where no one will find it. I am sorry I could not bring him home, but there was only me and I...just could not carry him all the way here. You may be very proud of him - he saved her life. Two Germans in the patrol died but only Pierre was lost. I wish I could have brought him home to you...but I brought this."

He extended his hand palm upwards. In it lay the gold ring Marie had given to her Pierre on their wedding day. Now it was all she had of him. The ring... and this farm.

Thierry looked at his aunt with the saddest eyes she had ever seen. "What do I do now, Tante Marie? *Maman* needs me and you need me. Where should I go? I want to help but I cannot be here with you and there with her too. What do I do?"

The stranger answered in her stead. He told Thierry he should stay with his *Tante* Marie until she decided what she would do, and then he gave his farewell and left the two of them together to sort out the shambles of their lives.

Later that day, Marie's neighbor came and took them both in his hay wagon to Langnac. It was decided that evening that Thierry would go back to Bergerac with his aunt and Robert would stay with Sandrine, who was numb with shock, and it was going to be difficult for all of them. But Marie could get by with Thierry's help with the orchards and Sandrine's neighbors and Robert could help her with their farm crops. At least for the time being that was how it would be.

Before he left, Thierry saw his friends Yves and Jean and told them, finally, everything that had happened. They had all changed from the children they'd been last week to...something else.

War does that. Death does that.

Thierry had lost both his father and his uncle, Sandrine and Marie their husbands. France had lost two good men.

And for what?

Linda Conn Amstutz

Chapter TWENTY-FIVE

September 9, 1995

Bellevue

As Clare's little car climbed the hill to our peaceful oasis at the top, Jean awoke. I had been thinking that both of them had had enough excitement for one day, and so I suggested that I would make some pasta and a salad and asked them both to come to my pigeonnier in about an hour and a half. They agreed.

I ambled up the path and opened the door to my little haven. I sat by the cold wood stove in the only comfortable chair and just "was" for a few minutes.

When I didn't think I could sit any longer I got up, snagged the chicken breasts from the freezer and put them in a saucepan of tepid water to thaw then searched through the fridge for something interesting to do with the pasta. I found some arugula and washed it, leaving it to drain on paper towels on the cupboard. Clare had left a basket of black walnuts atop the fridge so I shelled a few before I smashed a couple cloves of the lovely rose-colored garlic I'd bought at the market.

I made a salad of *feuille de chene* (red oak leaf) lettuce, and dressed it simply with walnut oil and lemon juice finally taking the nearly thawed double chicken breast from the water, drying it off with paper towels and slathered it with butter. Then I took my snips out to Clare's herb garden and cut some leaves of fresh sage. I snipped them into small pieces and rubbed them onto the butter, sprinkled on some salt and black pepper and stuffed the whole thing into the oven to roast.

Dessert would have to be a chocolate bar - there was nothing else in my nearly bare cupboard!

I filled a pot with water to boil for the pasta, poured myself a glass of pineau and sat down to reflect on this day's happenings.

I had been ready to poke all sorts of holes in Jean's story, and that wasn't what happened at all. I had listened, asked my questions and...I believed him.

He is a very kind and an apparently honorable man, and Clare's assessment of him seems to be accurate in spite of her emotionally skewed perspective. I am certainly not in love with him as she obviously is, but I do think he is telling the truth and doing the right thing. What would happen now, though?

We needed to talk with Yves and see if he has found any reference to this situation in his father's journals. It would be a tremendous help if there was something about the day when Thierry, the child, brought the painting to the church or where the money came from or what part old M. de Rastignac played if indeed he played a part at all. Perhaps his son, who now lives in the chateau, who bought the organ and had it installed into the church, knows something that he hadn't remembered when Jean spoke with him... Anything would be helpful.

Then there is the Russian workman who is also after the painting. Right now I'd like NOT to trade places with Yves - since he's the only link the Russian knows about to the painting.

The oven was exuding good chickeny aromas, the water was steaming and just on schedule Jean and Clare were walking through the door, glasses and a bottle of wine in hand. I put the pasta in to boil and began to sauté the garlic in a good dollop of olive oil. A couple of cheek *bisous* from each of them and we all sat around my little table. So far not much had been said but things seemed "right" once again on this hilltop.

I put some crackers in a tiny bowl and asked Jean if he had spoken with the *gendarmes*.

"Yes, I called them as soon as I got in the door. They want me to come by in the morning to talk with the officer in charge but they said they would be watching Yves' house and the church with special care and assured me he would be kept safe. I hope they can do that. I explained generally what I had been doing in

Paris and they seemed satisfied - at least for now they are."

Clare and Jean sat at my little table and I handed them plates and flatware and some plaid seersucker cotton napkins Clare had made for the *pigeonnier* years ago. Earlier, I'd wandered out into the meadow and cut some Queen Ann's Lace as a bouquet for the table - so it looked simple and elegant.

I checked the pot of boiling pasta, set the ticking-tomato-timer and stirred the garlic in the skillet and turned down the heat. We sat in companionable silence, munching on the salty crackers and sipping the cool white wine, each grateful in our own way for the ritual of cooking and eating together.

The pasta began to sputter, water flowing in bubbles over the edge of the pot. I rose and turned the flame down and, just for good measure, tested its doneness. It was perfect... It must have known it was done! I drained most of it in a colander in the sink, removed the chicken, all brown and fragrant from the oven, and then dumped the colander's contents (including about a quarter cup of pasta water) into the garlicky oil in the pan.

Jean exclaimed, "Alors! Does that smell delicious! How much longer will it be, shall I pour more wine?"

I told him it was nearly finished. Then I added a couple of double handfuls of fresh peppery arugula, some Parmesan cheese and the walnuts I'd shelled earlier. I gave them a toss in the hot garlicky pasta and we were ready for our feast!

Jean poured our glasses full again and we began. He, around mouthfuls of pasta, asked if I had any Calvados or perhaps some port.

"Why?"

He replied, "I spoke earlier to Yves and he said he might drop by later this evening for a digestif. If you don't have anything we can return to my house where I have a lovely bottle of port and some *Bleu d'Auvergne* and some ripe figs. There's no hurry, as he said it would be nearly nine o'clock before he would be here."

I checked my watch and discovered to my surprise - and Jean's also - that it was already a bit after eight!

"Ah. I'm afraid I have nothing – no Calvados or port. Shall we head to yours afterwards?"

So we finished our pasta and salad, put the dishes in the sink to soak and nearly waddled up the pathway to Jean's house. The sun had just set and the apricot afterglow made the world...just fine.

The timing was near perfect as we saw the lights of a car coming up the steep hill and turning on our lane just as we got to Jean's front door.

Jean opened it and flicked on some light switches, bathing both the outside of the house and the salon-cum-kitchen with a warm glow. Since the sun had gone down the evening had turned quickly chilly and we were glad of the warmth of the room.

After *bisous* all around, Yves followed us into the house and we all agreed that some port and cheese and a fig or two was what we wanted. Jean busied himself in the kitchen and with Clare's help opened the bottle of port and put some glasses and a board for the cheese on bamboo tray...

Yves and I settled ourselves like old friends (?) on the leather settee where he turned to me, his caramel-colored eyes pouring over me until I felt like an ice cream sundae. "How are you, Margaret? It is good to have Jean back safely, is it not?"

"Yes," I agreed, unable to put two words together, so strong was the effect of his gaze. What was he looking for? I leaned back, trying to relax and the gaze followed me.

"I was hoping for an opportunity to see you again. Our last outing, I think I detected, did not please you too much - the spiders and the cramped space. You were uncomfortable, no?"

"I was." THERE! Two words! I was doing better.

Not a sparkling conversation exactly, but...a start. Why did he continue to look at me like that...and what was keeping Jean and Clare? I felt like a thirteen-year-old. What had happened to my self confidence? My verbal skills? Gone!

I imagined that I could feel heat radiating from his body and I felt my face getting hot. I didn't have that much wine with dinner, only a couple of small glasses. I took a deep breath and with all the moxie I could muster, I asked, "How have you been, Yves? I am happy to see you again as well."

There, now. I made a sentence. Two.

Jean and Clare appeared on the other side of the cocktail table and set the tray on it with four heavy crystal port glasses, a small decanter and a board with a few figs and some blue-veined cheese that was smelling very nice as it came up to room temperature.

I took a breath, realizing I'd not been doing much of that since sitting down here.

"This looks lovely, Jean - where did you find the figs?" I asked.

"There is a tree behind this house, but actually, Clare picked them a couple of days ago and suggested they'd go well with the cheese and port."

The tray also held a stack of tiny plates and some cocktail napkins, as well as some crackers and a few shelled walnuts. Each of us took a plate, Jean put a slice of cheese, half a fig and a few nuts on them and poured some of the dark tawny-colored fortified wine in each glass. Without further conversation we sipped and tasted and almost as one we sighed - such and elegant combination of flavors and textures...

"This is very good, Jean," Yves said.

Jean looked at Yves with intensity, his eyes asking for a serious answer. "Have you seen him? The Russian?"

"Yes, at the *cafe* yesterday just before lunch. He has not shown up for work but hasn't, well, at least yesterday he hadn't, left Langnac. I should go to the *Gendarmerie* and report him, I suspect. What did you tell them? I've seen a couple of fellows who must be police, hanging around the church this evening."

"I told them everything - how you found the painting, where it came from, that I took it to Paris, what it is likely worth. All of it.

"I could see no advantage to keeping anything from them. If they are going to be able to help, they must have the facts. Tomorrow in the morning, Yves, you should go with me to the *Gendarmerie* and try to give a description of the Russian. Also, have you seen him with anyone else? I mean, does he have friends here or is he on his own? They asked me that and I did not know."

"I have seen him with no one. However, I don't think it's reasonable to assume he is alone. By now he could have contacted someone who might help him in his efforts - since we caused him to lose the trail of the painting the first day, he could have enlisted help. Do you know how much he heard, how much he understands about the painting? I presume he knows it is valuable." He paused thoughtfully. "Have you spoken with Thierry since your return from Paris?"

"I can answer that!" A voice from the silently opened front door resonated across the room. "And the answer is NO!"

The third part of this triumvirate strode into the room, eliminating the necessity for anyone to wonder why the three of them had stayed close friends through the years.

Yves and Jean rose and embraced the man who could only be Thierry. Holy cow! I'd thought Jean was attractive, in an understated sort of way, then Yves set my nerve endings a'jangling. Now Thierry came into the light and I thought a younger version of Maurice Chevalier - in my opinion, the quintessential Frenchman – stood before us.

"…and this must be the wonderful Margaret! Hello, I am Thierry Duranthon," he said as he took my hand and - yes – kissed the back of it.

"Clare, you are a marvel - to be so worried about Jean and still look so lovely. How are you, my dear?" Thierry intoned as he embraced the happy woman. "And how does it occur that I was not invited to this little *soirée*?" he added with just a whiff of a grin at Yves and Jean, and not waiting for an actual answer to his presumably rhetorical query…

"Now, bring me up to date, will you?"

And we did.

While we were talking, filling Thierry in, Jean had got him a glass, poured him some port and brought a plate for some cheese, figs and nuts.

"Enough of danger and intrigue - Margaret", Yves looked in my direction, "tell us about yourself. Are you here permanently, I hope? Jean had told me he was happy you were here, but I think not so happy as I am! How did you come to know Clare?"

No longer so tongue-tied, I replied, "I have known Clare since before she came to Europe. She lived in Fairton in Ohio, where I live, and was spirited off by Peter to sail the Mediterranean - about twenty-five years ago! We have known each other not so long as the three of you, but long enough, I think. I am here just for the rest of this month, then back to Ohio to complete the sale of my business (thank God) and then...I am not sure... There you have my life in a nut-shell!"

"And a lovely nutshell it is!" Yves smiled at me and I thought I'd hyperventilate!

What is going on with me? I do not hyperventilate over anything!

We settled into quiet conversation and I watched the three men. What a trio! Each was beautiful in his own way - Jean dark, with a wisp of <u>mustache</u> - not tall, but taller than Clare; Yves with a sandy/silver-haired ponytail and intense caramel-colored eyes, a tall, lanky almost gawky looking body and laugh lines in his face.

Then there was Thierry who was of medium height and had wavy light reddish-brown and silver hair, weatherworn wrinkles and light icy blue eyes that reminded me of my mother's. Well, sort of. They were different but all of a piece here in this room. Most of us after our teenage-buddy-years never again feel the bond these three have shared all their lives. How blessed they were!

I had finished my port and, while I could have gazed at Yves all night, I thought it was about time for me to retire to my *pigeonnier* and said so.

Yves was quickly on his feet and offering me his hand saying that he, too, needed to go and would walk me up the little rise to my place first. A frisson of - was it lust? - went through me as I agreed and we said goodnight to the rest.

The moon was a sliver, just above the horizon, a golden orange color and there was the usual over-abundance of stars accentuated by the absence of artificial light on this hilltop. We picked our way up the driveway and then along the stepping stones, positioned by someone with legs longer, I think, than mine.

I never seem to be able to get my pace the right length to find the next one without looking, and looking, under present circumstances, did little good. So stumbling along I made my way to my summer home and Yves followed, catching my elbow from time to time.

When we reached the door, I turned to Yves and thanked him for accompanying me this far and rose on my tiptoes, putting a hand on his shoulder for balance so that I might kiss him on his cheek.

Well, that was my intent, anyway. He turned his head just enough and it was his warm moist and so soft lips that met mine and the peck headed for his cheek became a kiss of some exceptional depth and intensity.

What was going on here? That wasn't what I'd planned...or was it? Warmth spread through my midsection.

I momentarily thought to ask him in...but if my intentions were exceeded again to the same degree I'd be in big trouble! Or would I? No.

"Goodnight, Yves," I said when I had caught my breath.

"When will I see you again, Margaret? Because I'd like to see you again."

Chapter TWENTY-SIX

Spring 1941

Near Bergerac, the orchard of Thierry's *Tante* Marie

Some things are the same everywhere. *Tante* Marie was up before the rooster crowed just like Thierry's *maman*. Marie was making noises in the kitchen and she imagined she heard Thierry's stomach growl in response. She did hear his feet hit the floor as he climbed out of the soft feather mattress in Tante Marie's loft above her own bedroom and climbed down the ladder.

"Good morning, Tante Marie."

"Good morning, Thierry," she replied, "Did you sleep well, my dear? Are you hungry?"

"Yes, I did, and I am very hungry."

Tante Marie would learn that boys Thierry's age always answer that question in the affirmative...but that would come.

"I thought today we would finish the pruning and then perhaps we could begin the weeding in the apricot orchard."

There was a fire in the stove and something bubbled in a pan on its surface. Tante Marie had made a porridge with oats and added some dried apricots to it for sweetness. She wanted so much for Thierry to be happy during his time here but wasn't sure just how to achieve that goal. And she really did need his help. The sweet porridge was a good beginning.

There was a sharp rap at the door and *Tante* Marie was startled by it. Thierry quickly ran to the door and opened it to the man who had come the day before yesterday, the one who brought the bad news about *Oncle* Pierre.

Marie saw Thierry step back, afraid of what this man might have to tell them now. There was no look of sadness about him today as there had been then…perhaps it would be fine.

"Madam, I thought you would like to know," he began and then waited for her to react before he went further. When she nodded, he continued, "I have confirmation that the package from day before yesterday was safely delivered to its destination in Catalonia without further incident. It, at least for the moment, is safe and out of harm's way."

Marie who didn't (by design) know the stranger's name, nodded again and said, "Thank you." He turned and left without any further conversation.

Marie, who had without knowing it, been holding her breath, let it out in a loud whoosh. She sat down at the table, put her head in her hands and shook it back and forth.

Her nephew got up and walked around the table to comfort his aunt. She knew he didn't know what he was supposed to do but felt he had to do something. There were only the two of them, and it was up to him to bring her comfort just as it was up to her to do the same for him when he needed it. She hoped she could do as good a job as he was doing now.

He put his arm around the back of her shoulders and asked quietly, "Is the "package" Annaliesa? Is she safely in Spain? Is that what he meant?"

"Yes, she is safe. Her safety was costly to us, but at least she IS safe."

"Will I ever see her again, Tante?"

"No, Thierry, probably not."

And they went on with their work.

Chapter TWENTY-SEVEN

September 10, 1995

Bellevue, the dark of the night

My head will not stop spinning. What have I done? I let him kiss me. No, I didn't "let" him do anything - I actively participated in the event. I have been thinking that I was glad to take a break from the "courting thing" with John and here I am stirring up something with this handsome (Ooo! too handsome) Frenchman. I should not do this. I cannot do this. Will not do this!

I'd known John for over a year before we got to this point in our relationship and I have spent all of about an hour with Yves – if you count all three of the times I have been in his presence. I must admit I thought him attractive looking from the very start, but still...

Hell! I am not really sure if he is married! If it were just the peck on the cheek I'd intended, being married wouldn't have made a difference, but that was a real kiss (oh, my, was it!) and if I were his wife...well, I wouldn't want to be his wife under these circumstances. But he is French and the French have different views about this sort of thing. I have been coming to France for over twenty years and never had to personally think of what Frenchmen do or do not do in situations like this... I guess the first thing I must do is find out whether or not Yves is married. Then I have to... Well, I have to think it through.

Think WHAT through? All he did was give me a... well...French kiss. I'm making a mountain out of a molehill here, right? What's one little kiss?

Little? It curled my toes. That was no little kiss. When you see a heroine in a movie go down the path toward...well, the wrong path... you want to scream to her "Don't open that door!, that is where I am at this moment and I am screaming at myself, "It's not too late!" Yeah, RIGHT.

Tomorrow I will ask Clare or Jean if Yves is married. Then I will decide what direction to go. Who am I kidding? I don't have any direction to go here. I have an understanding with John...sort of. I'd string him up by his thumbs if he were kissing some woman in Ohio at this moment! Wouldn't I?

The truth is that one of the good parts of our relationship is that the intensity is so dialed-back that I would probably be philosophical about it and "try to understand" what was happening if I knew he'd kissed someone. That is the truth! Now I am wondering...is this a good thing? Also, I guess I should wonder how he would feel if he knew I'd kissed Yves – livid or philosophical? Why am I afraid he'd be philosophical?

It was only a kiss.

Someone once told me, "Never trust your horizontal thoughts."

I'm going to sleep now and worry about this tomorrow.

Linda Conn Amstutz

Chapter TWENTY-EIGHT

Early Sunday Morning, September 10, 1995

Langnac

Because it was a Sunday morning and because I knew John planned to phone me about noon, I hopped on my bicycle as soon as I had my teeth brushed and clothes on and rode into Langnac for some exercise, a warm croissant from the bakery by the Post Office and a *"Grand Café Créme"* at the *café* by the marketplace where it was just as quiet this morning as it had been bustling on Friday. An English newspaper lay among the others on a table by the door of the cafe - The International Herald Tribune published in Paris. I took it and I settled into a wicker (well, plastic "wicker") chair outside the café to observe the world going by (not

278

much to see here) and to find out what, if anything, had changed outside this peaceful place.

I could sit here and gather all the crumbs left from my croissant and read the news and sip my coffee until the sun was nearly high in the sky before I had to climb on my bike and pedal back to Bellevue (a short 20 minute ride, but UPhill at the end) where I would talk on the phone with John and get back to "real" stuff.

This was pretty much what I did every Sunday while I was here and it was rather close to meditation, or stretching the point, worship. I was neither sufficiently fluent in French nor Catholic so going to Mass on a Sunday morning doesn't "do it" for me.

The English church - well, the circuit riding preacher from the Church of England - holds a service in Yves' *Église* de Notre Dame. They rent the building from the Catholics and hold their service on one Wednesday morning per month here in Langnac. I have truly enjoyed the English Church - the preacher is quite old fashioned but the little band of English speaking Christians (Dutch, Belgian, British and Indian Protestants) meet just as Christians have met, in small groups, since the very beginnings of Christianity. One Wednesday a month is fine with me, as long as I can have my coffee, croissant and quiet meditation here on Sunday mornings.

Conversation, loud conversation, behind me jerked me from my reverie! The young waiter was cowering before a burly guy speaking some language I didn't understand. Oh my, maybe it was Russian! I had turned around and glanced at the guy making the fuss and didn't much like what I saw. He was strong looking, if a bit soft around the middle, and he had dishwater blonde hair cut in what might be described as a crew cut - he looked, however, nothing like Dave Garroway. He was not handsome but rather brutish looking. He had a scar defining the pouch under his right eye - the left pouch had no such excuse. Apparently he didn't like whatever he had been served and was refusing to pay for it. I suspect this guy might be "our" Russian as I have not seen many others around Langnac.

I shook my paper and turned the page as though I was paying no attention to the argument behind me wishing I had brought my purse, rather than just the wallet in my back pocket, so I could powder my nose and look into the mirror of my compact. I watch too many spy movies, I guess.

Now they were making enough noise that anyone would turn and look, so I did. The burly Russian had apparently prevailed and the poor waiter looked defeated. The Russian walked up the hill to the main street - toward the church.

I quickly put coins sufficient to pay for my coffee and a tip for the young man, hopped on my bicycle. I rode toward the church on a parallel street to the one the Russian had taken. I wanted to warn Yves. It could have been that the big oaf wasn't heading that way at all but I thought in this case safe was better than sorry. I rode up to the back side of Yves house, threw my bike against the fence and rapped sharply on Yves' back door. It was still way too early for anyone to be coming to mass, but perhaps Yves had tasks there before the parishioners arrived. Whew! He was still here! He came to the door, fastening his jeans as he opened the door. I think I woke him.

"I just came from the cafe and a Russian guy was there abusing the waiter. When he left he was headed this way. I thought you'd like to have some warning!" I spluttered before I had caught my breath.

"…and good morning to you, Margaret!" He replied calmly.

"I really think we should call the *gendarmes* or something…" I babbled, more scared than I had been in a long time. This guy, the Russian, could be part of the Russian mob for all we knew, or at the very least an individual bully and he knew where Yves lived.

"Come in, Margaret, and we will see what this Russian will do." Yves said evenly. "I'll make us some coffee and we will visit until we see if he comes here…"

I left my bicycle against the fence and entered his very utilitarian kitchen, past the herbs growing on either side of the door. Where Jean's had been opulent and colorful, Yves was very basic but there was evidence everywhere that he used this room. There were herbs in string-tied bunches hanging from the rafters, the small four burner gas stove looked like it had had experience. There was a colander and several unpolished copper pots hanging from a steel rod against the wall near the stove. And there were several kind-of-leggy geraniums growing on the window sill over the large stone sink. The floor was terracotta in square tiles that had seen much traffic but were scrupulously clean as was everything else I could see: the scrubbed pine narrow rectangle of a table, next to a yellow sideboard with shelves above it, was surrounded by four mis-matched chairs that had been painted an egg yolk yel-low to match the legs of the table.

I sat in one.

I smiled as I recognized the pottery of Larry For-busher. He was the gangly white haired English ex-pa-triot potter from the Langnac market from whom I had also bought many lovely handmade dishes to take home to Ohio. I either gave his work as gifts to very good friends or kept on my own kitchen shelves. I am ashamed to admit I kept more than I gave away. Pot-tery is heavy enough that you need to like someone very much before you are willing to carry their gift 4000 miles through at least two airports - as I do not entrust pottery to the baggage handlers. "Do you know Larry Forbusher?" I asked Yves.

"*Ah, oui*! For many years, I have known him and also Dorothy when she was here. Too bad they couldn't stay together. His pottery is very nice but she was the better artist, I think, for the painting on the pottery."

I told him, "I rather like Larry's quirky farm animals, especially the joyful pigs and the sleek, stylized hares - oh, and his cocky roosters! Her geometric and botanical designs were quite attractive, but I think I like Larry's critters better!"

Here I was going on about his dishes when the Russian was lurking somewhere nearby. The thing was, I felt completely safe here in Yves kitchen and he didn't seem worried as he puttered about in his bare feet, making coffee and warming the milk. I examined the colorful unmatched plates in his sideboard while he poured the coffee and added (without asking) the hot milk to my cup as well as his.

He handed me my cup and sat in the chair adjacent to mine. I stirred sugar from a bowl of odd shaped cubes of raw sugar set in the middle of the narrow table. As I stirred and the sugar dissolved he turned his gaze upon me again.

"What were you doing in Langnac so early on a Sunday? Coming to mass?"

"No, just communing with the Herald Tribune at the *café*. I like your kitchen, Yves. It has such a comfortable, capable feel to it - do you cook more than coffee?" I wanted to know more about him and if he now told me that his wife cooked...well, that would cook his goose! At least for me it would.

"Yes, Margaret, I have always enjoyed to cook but I have had to do it more since my wife died."

Well, now I knew.

"Oh, Yves, I am sorry to hear you lost your wife. Was it long ago?"

"She died five ...no it is nearly six years ago now. She died giving birth to my son, who also died. It was a horrid time, but life has gone on and I am fortunate to have fine friends who helped me through the worst times - still do. I have had my work and Jean has returned to Langnac and Thierry is nearby...Life continues and one must also...continue."

Well, this isn't something I had expected. I was still for a time then looked at his lovely eyes, reached for his hand which was on top of the table and covered it with mine and said "Yves, I am so sorry. It must have been hard for you. Do you have other children?"

"No. I have only my work and my friends, among whom I hope I may count you!"

"Of course you may."

Some time passed, I don't know if it were seconds or minutes. We sat there forming our new friendship - our hands together on the well scrubbed tabletop.

When it seemed time to talk again, I asked "Have you looked at the records your father kept to see if you can learn anything about the painting, or where the money came from that your father gave to the girl?"

Before he had an opportunity to answer, there was a knock at the front door of the house - I had completely forgotten why I was there and it all came rushing back into my consciousness. A jolt of finger-tingling fear caused me to jerk my hand away from his and we looked at each other - both thinking that it could be the

Russian…but would he knock? Perhaps it was some-one else…

Yves rose and walked slowly through the door to the hallway to look out the window and see who might be at the front door. I heard him open the door and begin talking with someone. I couldn't hear clearly and my understanding of his French isn't trustworthy but I think he said:

…No, I have not seen him but my friend has. She came here a few minutes ago to alert me of his presence…"

Soon both the young gendarme and Yves came into the kitchen. Now, we conversed in English "Here she is" - begun by Yves (for my benefit) and continued then by the cop. "Where, madame, did you see this man?"

"Well, to begin with, I am not really certain it is the same man who caused the trouble the other day…I only guessed that it was by both his language and by his surly and unpleasant manner. I saw him having a dispute with that dear young waiter at the café about half an hour ago. He left without paying and he was headed this way; so I stopped to alert Yves."

"Ah." he said stroking his chin and looking for all the world like a movie police detective.

Slung over his shoulder was a well worn canvas and leather bag, like a messenger bag, from which he extracted a small computer. As he removed it from the bag he asked Yves and then me if we could describe the man to him. As we spoke, he tapped on the keyboard and our disjointed descriptions slowly became a face - broad face with some pock marks from what might have been acne, small eyes set rather far apart, blue...no, more greenish hazel eyes, tawny-colored hair that was short-cropped into a "flattop", high cheekbones, that scar below his right eye, sparse eyebrows, thin lips and a nose that had seen some fighting. It was crooked from having been broken, maybe more than once. He was probably in his middle to late thirties and neither short nor tall - yes, yes, less than six feet but stocky. When he turned the laptop around for us we saw the face that was too narrow by a bit, but it was certainly the Russian thug Yves had dealt with - AND the man I saw in the *café*. He quickly broadened the face and it could have been a sketch of the man made as he posed across the table from us, the likeness was so accurate! Of course we didn't know his name but this was surely a beginning. His work done, the policeman thanked us for our help and was gone as abruptly as he had come.

I looked at my watch as the morning had included much more than my coffee and croissant and saw that I needed to get back to Bellevue before the appointed hour of John's phone call. I'd make it but with not much time to spare. "Yves, I must get back to Bellevue, thank you for the coffee and I hope I will see you again before I leave."

Yves looked my way. For a beat or two he said nothing. Then, the hesitation making his words more consequential, he said, "Margaret, I very much hope to see a great deal of you before you leave, if indeed you leave at all." And he smiled.

"Wha..." I looked at my watch again, not really wanting to have this conversation now or maybe at all and said "Gotta go!"

Often physical exercise clears the mind, sometimes it simply allows one to not think at all and sometimes it muddles everything. This was an example of the latter.

I had wanted to clear my head before I spoke with John and as it happened, by the time I got to Bellevue I was more confused, much more confused.

I have been busy making judgements about poor Clare's ability to think clearly about Jean and here I was - with equally confused thoughts but this time I was on the inside looking out instead of the outside looking in!

I barely knew this man, Yves Menton. I liked the way he looked, I would even say I have enjoyed a frisson of attraction for him since the first time I laid eyes on him. And it wasn't just looks, he was sweet and sexy and seemed trustworthy and he obviously felt some attraction for me, or at least he wanted me to believe he did. Was that just a "Frenchman" thing? Did they all behave charmingly and as though the woman to whom they are speaking was very attractive to them...? Many did, I think, but this one?

John had treated me well and behaved as though I were someone special to him. He was considerate and gentlemanly. He was consistent in his affection and did not flirt with other women. Actually, being a preacher is sort of mutually exclusive to being a flirt. Funny, I hadn't thought about it but both of them are involved with the church.

That little electric thing that Yves ignites in my midsection has never been a factor in my friendship with John. I have considered that a favorable feature, until now. I'd really forgotten how good it felt. I like it. My head certainly knows that "chemistry" is not a firm foundation for a relationship - but it is a nice adjunct to the whole package. What was I thinking? Couldn't this be what an official marriage contract was all about? Is this a test? When you have a perfectly good relationship and you meet someone who stirs your "chemistry" - how do you handle it?

Temptation.

How strong was our relationship, John's and mine? Should I simply have looked at Yves as Adam should have looked at Eve and said..."No, no apple for me, thanks!"

...Or was this a wake up call for me to rethink where I was going with John. If what John and I had were strong - why was I attracted to Yves at all? I really wanted to have time to have thought this through before I talked with John but now it was 11:45 AM and I pedalled for all I was worth to get there before the phone rang.

Linda Conn Amstutz

Chapter TWENTY-NINE

Late Sunday Morning

Bellevue

Breathing like a smoker after a marathon and perspiring until my teeshirt was clinging to my back, I leaned my bicycle against the wall of the pigeonnier, went inside and trudged up the stairs. Partly I wanted to splash some cold water on my face and partly because upstairs was where the phone jack was. Clare's spare phone was up there too and it still needed to be plugged in!

The water felt really good as I made a cup of my two hands and both rinsed my face and slurped some of the welcome cold liquid. No time was left to dawdle over the sink though - the phone rang.

"Hello?"

"Oh, Marg, it is so good to hear your voice, Hon! How are you? What have you been up to? Did you find that guy who went missing? Are you OK? I mailed you a letter yesterday - a short one, but at least I sent it. Are you there? Marg?"

"Gee, John, take a breath and I'll try to answer some of your questions! I am fine, a little out of breath my-self as I just dragged my bicycle up the big hill. I swear it seems to get steeper every year! Other than that all is well here, and yes, we did find Jean. Er, he found us. He phoned from Paris and we picked him up at the train station in Bordeaux last evening. Let's see, what else did you ask?

"How are you doing? How's it going in Coalville? Have you got your sermon finished for this morning?"

He'd probably made a list of questions to ask. I was just winging it...and not that well.

"Of course my sermon's finished, and everything's fine here except that I am missing you like crazy.

Where was that guy? Do you know what happened to him?"

"Jean was in Paris. He took a very valuable painting there for his friend, who is an art dealer, to appraise. He'd left with Thierry in a huge hurry because they thought a Russian thug was after the painting. As it turned out, the Russian followed Yves, so Jean and Thierry were in no danger, but they didn't know it at the time. The police are looking for the Russian now but I saw him at the café just this morning!" I related to him.

"You didn't go to church this morning?"

"No, remember, the English church is on Wednesday here in Langnac, and only once a month at that. I was meditating over my coffee and *croissant*, though. I have not become a heathen…yet."

"Um…Eve, who's she and who's Terry?" John asked very quietly.

"HE. Yves is a he. He and Thierry are Jean's child-hood friends. Yves is also the *sacristan* of the church in Langnac - sort of like Mark is the custodian at your church, only, I think, a little bit more responsibility even. His father was *sacristan* before him and it was in the church where they discovered the painting hidden in a wall. We think Yves' father is the one who hid it there, but we are still working on that. I'll keep you posted. Oh, and Thierry grows wine grapes near Bergerac."

"Are you having fun?" John queried.

"Sure! It hasn't been as restful a time as it usually is, but it feels good to be here and I am really glad poor Clare didn't have to go through this all on her own. The *gendarmes* are on the job now and I am confident we are quite safe, although I will feel better when they find the Russian guy!"

"Do you miss me, Marg?" John asked, suddenly serious.

"John, of course I miss you, but this is a good time for me to do some mental adjustments. Because of selling the agency, I need time to get adjusted to that idea and to what I want to do next in my life, when I don't have twenty employees depending on me and payables to worry about and customers to satisfy. I have fulfilled my responsibility to the bank and to my

investors and now I am going to do something different... I just don't know what yet. It isn't as though I
have no choices – I have too many."

"For what it's worth, I know what I want you to do
next. I want——"

"Stop right there, John! Just give me this time to get
my thoughts straightened out, will you, please? I have
a lot going on in my head right now - let me sort it all
out, please."

I was trying to sound reasonable and not scared but
I think he was near to saying something I really wasn't
ready to deal with. I need to take things one step at a
time. John is a very good fellow - but I think, if I let
him, he might take advantage of this time of transition
in my life, when I am vulnerable, and try to persuade
me to do something that might be what he wants but
that I might regret later on. I have been single a very
long time. I'm not at all sure I want to change that!

"All right, Marg, so tell me more about these guys
Yves and Thierry. Should I be worried? Are they married? Oh, Sweetheart, I wish you'd never left home. I
feel so far away and you sound...different."

"Don't worry about me, John. I can fend for myself. To answer your question: Yves is a widower and I am not sure about Thierry, but certainly they should cause you no worry."

Now I was treading on thin ice.

"It is lovely to hear your voice," I continued, "but I am thinking this phone call is getting expensive. Soon as I get your letter I will answer it and send my reply back lickety-split. I promise! Take care, Sweetie."

"Ok, I'll look for your letter... I miss you so, Marg, I love you."

And then there was a click and he was gone. He didn't wait for me to repeat a vow of love returned - or perhaps he was afraid I wouldn't.

I unplugged the spare phone and plodded down the stairs, opened the refrigerator and grabbed an apple, some cheese and an open bottle of white wine. I took this luncheon picnic and the book I was reading and headed for the stone table in the shade between our houses, bent upon escaping into a fictional world where the outcome of the story can be found by simply reading the last chapter. Not that I would do that, of course...but I could if I really wanted to know. Not so with my life - too many variables. And I suppose I don't really want to know the ending anyhow...

"Want some company or just peace and quiet so you can read your book?" Clare came around the corner of her woodshed with a napkin wrapped around a sandwich in one hand and a mug of some indeterminate beverage in the other.

"Company would be good...and yours in particular would be great! I just got off the phone with John. I think I discouraged him just as he was beginning the groundwork of a proposal."

Clare looked at me a little sideways, "A 'proposal' proposal or just something else?"

"I am afraid absence has made - well, you know - and while I am very fond of John, I am going in so many different directions just now, I really don't want to have to answer 'the question'...or not answer it. I just don't want him to ask it until I get settled enough to have an answer. It might be easier once the agency deal is finished. For sure I'm too young to knit sweaters in a rocking chair for the rest of my life." I said, laughing at the idea. "But I don't want to decide anything for a while - I just want to get the responsibility off me and be able to breathe for a while without worrying about payroll and deadlines and phone messages. It seems John sees this as an opportunity and he doesn't want to let it pass...or he's afraid to let it pass. I really hope he doesn't push. I will say 'No' if he pushes."

"Smart girl, Marg. You know exactly what is best for you... T.I.M.E. And if he's the right guy, he'll understand that."

"So, on another subject, how much do you know about Yves Menton?"

"Not much. Jean thinks the world of him. He does a good job for the church. The priest is seldom there. It seems he has several villages he serves so Yves pretty much does everything but say the Mass. I think he even does some counseling. Before he came back to Langnac, while his father was still *sacristain*, Yves worked as a clinical psychologist in Bordeaux - and he kind of burned out there just about the time his dad got sick. He came here to help his dad and decided he likcd the work and when his father died, he just stayed on. His wife was a local girl - younger by quite a bit - and they weren't married long. Yves was a late bloomer, according to Jean, and when he finally decided to get married and have a family the result was disastrous. He has borne up well, I think, but it was an awful blow to lose his wife, she died in childbirth, the baby too. It was one ghastly day."

"He told me this morning that his wife and child had died when the child was born."

"You saw Yves this morning? Where did you see him? Did you go to mass?" Clare asked, clearly amazed.

"Nope, actually I was at the *café* and I saw a man I suspected to be that Russian jerk. When he left, I went to warn Yves - the Russian was headed in his direction when he left the *café* - then Yves made me some coffee and we had a short chat. It was just getting interesting when the *gendarme* knocked on the door. He asked us a few questions then he made a sketch of the creep on his computer... Clare, it was amazingly accurate! Plus we determined that the guy I saw at the cafe IS the same guy who tried to get the painting from Yves and Thierry. I guess it is good to know that there is only one of them."

"You've had an interesting morning!" Clare said when I'd finished, her voice full of admiration. "Why'd you ask what I knew about Yves?"

"I don't know. I think he is bright and attractive, and, Oh! by the way…French…and he has the nicest eyes… Just askin', I guess. It doesn't hurt to know about a guy. Right?"

"Hmmm," hummed Clare.

Chapter THIRTY

Sunday afternoon

Église de Notre Dame, Langnac

Yves, finished now with the regular Sunday tasks required of him by his job, went from the sanctuary into the small office of the *sacristain*. The room was lined on two walls with bookshelves, and while there were a few other items there, most of the shelves were occupied by books, leather-bound, some musty, of varying sizes. All contained the workaday history of the parish, the *Église* de Notre Dame.

Much of the history was in the form of ledgers detailing the collections from each mass and the separate

gifts to the church by parishioners who made memorial donations, or donations made at the time of a bap-
tism or a wedding, and rents paid by the protestants
using the building on Wednesdays. On the other side
of these ledgers were monies sent to Rome, amounts
spent for the salary of both the priest and the sacristain, purchase of the vestments worn by the priest,
candles, repairs to the church edifice itself, to the recto-
ry and to the *sacristain's* little house, additions to the
church building and the two houses and expenses for
festival days and such holiday preparations as came
along. Much about the life of the church might be
learned by following the trail of income and outgo of
funds, as is true of any family or business.

Also on these shelves stood other books from the
long history of Langnac's only church. Each *sacristain*
kept a parish register, a record of things not adequately
defined by *francs* and *centimes*. Some of her *sacristains*
were reluctant writers: while they were required to
scrupulously keep the ledgers, some simply didn't
record much else. Both Yves and his father, Louis, liked
to tell the story of their little church and its parish-

ioners, and so kept careful daily records of the goings on both of the church and the village. It was for this reason that Yves had set aside this afternoon for looking through the parish register and ledgers with the firm conviction that he had a good chance of discovering more about the little painting of the Madonna and how it came to be inside the wall behind the new organ. He hoped also to find from what source had come the money given to the little Jewish girl as she made her way to sanctuary in Spain.

Yves was a particularly organized fellow as was his father, and to be truthful, his job as sacristain was a good deal less demanding of his time than his last job and he had the opportunity to keep the little office in perfect order, and he did. He easily found the ledger and parish register from 1941, sat at the desk and began to read.

It was a disturbing story that he found.

The parishioners in 1941 had no money and so the church had no money. The Third Reich had appropriated whatever they wanted or needed from wherever they found it with no thought for those who had grown or made or bought it. The children, particularly those in the town, were hungry - and if the children were hungry, their parents were starving. The weekly collections had dwindled to almost nothing. If it hadn't been for M. de Rastignac, the owner of the chateau, both the priest and Yves' family would have starved. The times had been grim. No repairs were made to the building, save those which required only the skill of his father and the tools at hand.

What Yves found in the parish register, however was another story entirely. The incidents of heartwarming care and Christian compassion he read kept him sitting at the desk for an indeterminate period of time...he was enthralled and learned a great deal both about his papa and the people of this village.

Certainly there were tales of treachery, like the seven townsmen who were betrayed to and summarily shot by the Germans, simply because they were accused of having sold gasoline to the partisans. There was never any trial, no proof, just an accusation. The Germans "made an example" of them to frighten anyone else who might consider such a crime. Today there is a marker designating the spot where the massacre occurred which reads, "Here seven men of the village were murdered by the Germans March 26, 1941". It is just up the hill from the church. He walked by it every day without thinking of those families...now he did.

Then there was the day when his papa wrote tersely of the death of his lifelong friend, Thierry's father, Roland Duranthon. The bare facts were all his papa could bring himself to record, unlike the stirring detail Louis used when he described the loving way the village came together to support the seven widows whose husband's names where on the memorial.

There was nothing but the simple fact of Roland's disappearance and no mention of a funeral or of where he had been laid to rest. Yves wondered if it were simply too painful for his papa to write or if it were something more. Had he been involved in the tragedy or in the sequence of events which happened before or after it and dared not write it here in this quasi-public document?

The more Yves read, the more he noticed other times when there were far fewer details than some of the narratives held. Yves wondered. His papa seemed to need to write of the facts of this village's life in a way that kept them for those in later generations to understand, and yet from time to time he simply glossed over a seemingly important occurrence with virtually no detail at all.

Could there be another document?

When he came to the place, the one just before the disappearance of his friend (and then the death of Roland's brother the following day) when there should have been some mention of the painting, some description of how he had handled the transaction that produced the young girl's "traveling money" there was nothing! It was Louis to whom Thierry had given the painting. Thierry had told Yves and Jean that day when he left to live with his aunt on her farm in Bergerac. That day that had changed their little triumvirate to a duo since Thierry was never back in Langnac for long; an odd visit now and then. But nothing was ever the same.

Why was there no mention of it at all? There were excruciating details about day to day events like the

Saumet family and their bout with influenza when, having virtually nothing to eat themselves, several other families – the Dosiles, the Courcelles, and the Sussacs – brought a meal to the Saumets each day until all of them had recovered. "Surely, God's hand at work here on earth," Louis had observed.

And there were other times he noted acts of Christian sacrifice and love - Madame Dupuy who had a very difficult time with the birth of her daughter. Her husband had been one of the seven killed to set the example. She gave birth but could not care for either herself or for the child, so Mesdames Bertrand and Sussac took turns sitting with her, feeding the baby and her, until she was again strong enough to manage on her own. Both she and the child surely would have perished without the help of her friends, his papa had recorded.

Yves read example after example and yet no mention at all was made of the painting. He looked up and realized it had become dark - he had been here the whole of the afternoon and found virtually nothing.

There was one more thing he thought to do before going back to his house and fixing some supper. Now that he had determined just what date Thierry's father had died, he knew where to search in the ledger book to see what he might find. When he'd looked before he knew it was in the spring, but not the exact date.

April 16, 1941.

Yves grabbed the ledger for 1941 from the shelf and opened it to the page for April 16 – and he was really surprised by what he found there.

Chapter THIRTY-ONE

Early Sunday evening

Home of the *sacristain*, Langnac

Yves walked back across the garden path to his kitchen door murmuring to himself, "No, that simply doesn't make sense. Every other Sunday there is an entry for the collection, however meagre, in the ledger, yet nothing at all on that Sunday." Nothing. Not a *sou*.

There was no entry for that day at all. The previous and following days each had small expense notations but nothing about the collection income for Sunday. He had checked for a month or so before and following April and then looked through to the end of the year and there were always entries for Sunday's offering. Always.

Of course there may have been nothing collected. But NOTHING? On some other Sundays, several in fact, the amounts were as small as ten francs. One was even three francs. But nothing? Because of what Yves knew about that particular day, the other events that occurred, he tried to believe otherwise, but he knew - his papa had given the church's money to the girl! It was so unlike him to be anything but scrupulously honest with the church's funds. How much had the collection been that day? Had M. de Rastignac been in attendance? The days when he attended were notable because there was a large collection on those days. It was how the priest and Yves' family survived.

Yves felt like a forensic accountant. With a sigh, he turned and walked, his stomach making hungry growls, back to his office in the church and picked up the ledger again. He looked again at the Sunday after and found a fairly large collection. Had M. de Rastignac been there? Or had papa replaced the money he'd taken the Sunday before? No notations existed in the ledger or the parish register on either the 16th or the 23rd of April, 1941.

Eventually, Yves returned to the house, poured himself a glass of white wine from the bottle in his refrigerator and looked around for something to cook for his supper. Such things as these are hard to deal with on an empty stomach and his, he realized, was very empty. He found a cabbage and some local garlic sausage and chopped the cabbage, plopping it in a pan with a dollop of butter and a splash of the wine from his glass. Then, he put the sausage on top of the cabbage and a lid on the pan and put the combination on the stovetop to cook. Supper was an abbreviated affair - the cabbage and sausage would fuel his body but his mind was elsewhere.

About six or seven years ago, before his papa died, Yves had been living here in this house with him through his illness, having gratefully left his counselling practice in Bordeaux to tend him. Bordeaux is a good sized city and a port and his clientele had become increasingly from the Algerian and Moroccan immigrant community (funded by the national health plan) and he felt he had so little in common with his clients that he was increasingly less able to see positive outcomes. He achieved, finally, so little satisfaction from the job he had loved when he first began practicing that the end was easy. His father became ill and Yves found it convenient to simply resign from the clinic and come to Langnac to be a caregiver for his ailing parent. It was good to get to know his papa again – he'd been busy and just far enough away that he'd visited seldom during his counselling years.

Then his papa died and there was no one to care for the church. Of course, Yves had been doing his papa's work in the last months because Louis couldn't, so he knew the job. It suited him. It was different - more physical and much less stressful and frankly, he didn't need much money with the house provided by the church and his simple style of life. He liked it here and the parishioners liked him, so when they shyly asked if he could possibly stay on until they found a new sacristain he said he would like to have the job himself if they'd have him! They would and they did.

He had moved the few things he had from his apartment in Bordeaux and had put some of his papa's things in the attic – and had begun his life again!

He had met Adrianne before Louis' death and she had been sweet to him and helped him through his time of grieving. She cared for him in an honest, straightforward way that felt very right to him, and in spite of the difference in their ages he slowly fell in love with her. She'd been ill as a child and the illness had weakened her heart. When she was pregnant all sorts of difficulties arose, both with her and the baby, but Yves was so happy to be having a family he found it hard to imagine a bad result.

Neither Adrianne nor the baby survived the process of birth. Both were gone and Yves life simply halted. He worked and that was all. Then, after a couple of years of simply existing, going about his daily chores in a fog of loneliness and regret, the fog began to lift. His childhood friend, Jean, came back to Langnac look-ing for a house for his retirement. Yves helped him find one and gently Jean drew him out of the burrow in which he'd been hibernating. The two of them, Yves and Jean, formed a critical mass and drew Thierry into their childhood trio again. Thierry began visiting and the three of them were together again almost like when they'd been boys. Better even, it was now because all three had had experience and they realized how precious their friendship, their trust of each other, their bond truly was. All three were strengthened and healed - each in his own way - by their reunion.

Now, what had it been that started Yves trotting down this trail of memories?

Ah! It was Papa's trunk in the attic! The trunk was an old humpback affair with leather straps. It had been at the end of his bed, sort of "in the way" in the small bedroom. Yves had no use for it since it appeared to be full of all sorts of things, clothes, some small boxes and books, so he couldn't put any of his stuff in it. He had moved it, with the help of Jean and Thierry to the attic. He and Adrianne had made this their home and Yves was familiar with the contents of the shelves in the salon and the bedroom but he really didn't know what was in the trunk. Maybe…

He rummaged around in the kitchen until he found a flashlight and took it with him up the attic stairs at the far end of the hallway. He lifted the latch and pried open the seldom-used door. It was stuck but with an extra yank finally came open. He climbed the rest of the way, brushing the webs of the attic spiders out of his hair and smiled as he remembered how Margaret had shuddered as he'd burnt away the spiderwebs in the church's fortifications. He found the trunk and squatted before it, undoing the leather straps. It was full almost to the top. He discovered that there was a tray about 10 inches deep that lifted out. Yves lifted the tray by the leather handles on either end and set it carefully on the attic floor. The tray held garments - mostly Sunday clothes, not work duds. Underneath them lay a few framed photographs and the family Bible that Yves had known had to be somewhere, but had not been able to find. He put that aside to take downstairs. Explaining why the trunk was so heavy, beneath the tray he found a stack of leather-bound books tied together with cotton kitchen string. They were all the same size, but of varying ages, he judged by the coloration of the leather bindings. No words were stamped on the spines. Yves set them down in a tall pile and gently untied the string. He opened the top book and instantly recognized the handwritten script as that of his father. The title page read:

Louis Menton

1986-

Yves opened the next book and found it was dated 1984-1985 . So there were two years in each volume. He kept opening books until he hit pay-dirt:

Louis Menton

1940-1941

He put the 1940-1941 volume on the top and carried the whole pile along with the Bible, down the stairs, holding the flashlight in his mouth. He shoved the door closed with his foot and it latched itself, then he carried the treasure to the kitchen where he pushed his dishes aside, put the pile on the table and then, finally, walked out the back door and brushed the webs from his hair and shoulders.

Back in the kitchen, he sat and leafed through the pages until he began to see how his father had recorded his life. It was continuous. There were no new pages for a new day, not even a new line - the date simply divided one day from the next and the narrative continued. His papa had consistently noted things like remarkable weather, births and deaths in the village, the results of elections - both local and national – and a few stray opinions about them. There were notations about particularly fine meals and also the other kind. It was simply his life. Yves was touched by how deeply pleased his papa had been that he had decided to leave Bordeaux and come back to Langnac to help him. But soon Yves shook himself out of this wallow he'd been taking in the life of his papa and he found again the book containing the Sunday in April 1941 when M. Duranthon had been killed and when the dark eyed girl had given Thierry the tiny painting of the Madonna to sell in the village. To sell to the church? To sell to the *signeur*? To whom?

His hands were not sure of themselves as he opened the book and leafed through the winter and early spring notations. As he approached the date in question he began to read more about the activity of his

papa and Roland Duranthon and Arnauld Bertrand:
clandestine forays into the night with downed English
pilots, frightened Jewish refugees, exposed French partisans headed toward the Spanish border. He read
words his father never intended anyone else to read,
words describing fear that even today Yves could nearly smell.

His papa made several trips to the nearby village of
Challerville to the shop of a printer who in his back
room became the forger of the documents for these
contraband "packages" that needed delivery to Spain.
Three of these short journeys to Challerville had been
made in the week preceding the Sunday in question
and his panic grew with each successive one. The girl
had been with the Duranthons, hidden in their barn,
for nearly a week and each day she was there was
more terrifying than the last. If she were found by the
soldiers of the Reich the Duranthons would be held up
as examples and killed very publicly as had been the
seven who had been suspected of selling gasoline to
the partisans. Possibly even those who might be con-

sidered their friends would face the same fate. His father had been truly terrified.

And then he wrote:

"God forgive me for I have done the unthinkable! I have compromised the trust placed in me by the people of this parish and by the Holy Mother Church. I have sinned beyond my imagining! But that poor, probably-orphaned child, she had a tiny painting of the Madonna and she was told by her father, a dealer in art, to trade it to get money to save her life. The son of Roland and Sandrine, Thierry, came to me with the painting and there was no time to do anything else! I took it. I took all the money that had been in the collection plate and sent it with Thierry to the girl. At least, when she gets to Spain, she won't be penniless as well as alone. God forgive me."

For the remainder of that week Louis had recorded that, not only had his dear friend Roland been shot and killed in the woods but also Roland's brother Pierre had died on the route to Spain with the girl. He did say however that it had been reported that the girl arrived safely in Spain. She had been left with a family in a remote mountain village who had promised to keep her safe - if they could.

"**This war must end!**" he wrote "**Two of our tiny cell of passeurs** (guides for refugees) **has died, and we barely can do the work we set out to do with only the few of us that is left. I have heard that the Americans are coming, but who can tell? If they are coming why have they waited so long? So many have died, so many have been taken in the 'releve' to work in the German factories: all the men from 18-50 and single women from the age of 21-35! What is left of my France these days? She is full of starving people and crawling with Germans. If it weren't for my dearest Marie and my precious Yves...I could not, would not go on.**"

Yves had heard much about the war from the older villagers, but never had he felt its real horrors like he did now reading his papa's private words. He hesitated before turning the next page.

He knew what was coming.

Chapter THIRTY-TWO

Monday morning

Home of the *sacristain*, Langnac

Yves awoke, aching all over, his head lying on his right forearm on the scrubbed pine surface of the kitchen table top. The sun was coming in the glass panes of the door to the garden and he could hear chatter of children as they walked past his house. It was 8:15. The children went by at this hour every morning on their way to school.

The musty smelling leather-bound books were still stacked beside the one open book before him. He remembered. He had not had the courage to continue reading.

He, who was the son of this man who had many times risked his life in that war which was described on these open pages. "What a pathetic excuse for a man!" Yves thought of himself. His papa had lived it and had the courage to write it into these books and Yves couldn't bring himself even to read it. Pitiful - but he knew <u>this</u> story. Papa had told him this story. He knew how the RAF pilot had hidden in the garage of the empty gasoline station and how the Germans had searched for and finally found him. Yves knew the pilot had fought for his life, had shot and killed three of the German soldiers before he'd been killed himself. The local German commander had been white-hot with fury and grabbed the first three villagers he had seen. These villagers, three women, had been guilty of nothing more than standing on the street at that moment. They were made into examples. Dead examples. Mme. Disgoulliere, Mme. Pradeau and his dear mama shot for all to see, so that no one would dare defy the German.

Yves, in spite of his feeling like a coward, skipped the next few pages to the following Sunday, the day of the unusually large collection, and found what he had hoped for. His papa had gone to M. de Rastignac and asked him to buy the little painting "from the church" as it was valuable and M. de Rastignac was a collector of art. The desperation must have shown in his papa's eyes because the signeur gave his papa more francs than his papa had given the girl, plus his normal contribution. All was well, but that didn't explain the presence of the painting in the hollow wall...

Yves read on:

"M. de Rastignac has saved my soul! He didn't want to carry the painting into the mass and so left it with me for safekeeping until after the service when he came into my sacristy as I was putting away the vestments and the holy oils. He surprised me, as I am unused to anyone entering the sacristy...but he did.

He closed the door and silently slid the lock across, ensuring we would not be seen or heard. Then he asked me to see the painting and I handed it to him. Silently he gazed at it almost as a departing lover

looks upon his beloved. I know that feeling, having buried my dear Marie just this week. One last look - but surely he would take the painting now that he had given the money. However he looked up and said "She stays here. It is much less likely that the Germans will ravage this place than the chateau. Any day now they could decide to garrison troops there or move at least the officers from Siorac to Langnac and of course, they would want the chateau. No, she should stay here, safe in the sanctuary of God's house where she truly belongs. Please, Louis?"

"Of course, sir, I will find a place that is safe for her to stay."

So that is what I did. I hollowed out a space in the wall and put her in there. Then I plastered over the hole and painted over that. Our Madonna is safe. The place is a secret known only to me so that no one can compromise her safety. Surely I will not. Thanks be to God for this fine man, M. de Rastignac and for my salvation by his hand."

****

And this is what Marg saw when she peered in through the glass in the door of his kitchen: Yves, sitting at the narrow table, his head in his hands, sobbing over some old leather bound volumes. She rapped lightly on the glass and Yves looked up, wiped his face with his palms and smiled at her. He stood and walked to the door to let her in. She took his face in her hands, then they embraced. They held each other without knowing exactly why, only that it seemed right.

"They found him, the Russian," she reported. "He was charged with theft for leaving the café without paying. They found he was here illegally so he is in the gendarmerie now but will be sent back to Russia. He won't be tried for the theft, simply deported, but he dare not come back or he will be arrested."

"That is good news, Margaret. Would you like some coffee? Then I will tell you what I have found..."

Linda Conn Amstutz

Chapter THIRTY-THREE

September 1995, Monday afternoon

Bellevue.

Margaret

I'd filled Clare in about the documents Yves had uncovered...all of them. She listened and asked questions and finally was satisfied that all was finally well here in this peaceful place. We had made a pot of tea which had cooled while we talked and she had set about heating some more water when we heard a car on the lane and then turn into the courtyard of Bellevue. We looked first at each other then went to the window to see who it might be.

"Who's that?" Clare asked as a man, familiar to me but not to her, emerged from the little rental car.

I looked at her but my mouth didn't seem to want to work... Finally I spluttered... "It's John!"

"Jean who?" she asked.

"No, not Jean... JOHN! My John! What is he doing here?" I asked no one in particular as I walked to Clare's front door to go out and see if my eyes were indeed deceiving me or the preacher from Ohio who barely was inclined to drive the half hour to Fairton from Coalville had indeed crossed the Atlantic in an airplane and found his way to this rural hilltop in southwestern France all on his own! And WHY???

"John? Is that really you? How did you get here? What are you doing here? Is everything OK?" I asked, suddenly fearful of some disaster at home that couldn't be adequately communicated on the telephone.

"Hi, Sweetheart! I finally found you! You have no idea - no, I have no idea where I have been looking for Bellevue!" He enfolded me in his arms and whispered into my hair, "Oh, how I have missed you! I am so glad to see you! I do love you so!"

I took him, perhaps a bit roughly, by the shoulders and looked at his face...into his eyes. "What are you doing in France? What's wrong? How did you get here? Who's taking care of the church in Coalville? What is happening here?"

His eyes clouded and he said, "You're not glad to see me."

"Yes, of course I am! But I am just so surprised. Is everything all right at home? What is going on?"

"Everything is fine at home. I missed you so and I haven't had a real vacation in over four years, and you sounded so...strange on the phone. So I talked with the Council and they said it was fine to take a few days so...I did. And I came to the only place I wanted to be and that was here - with you! It's a good thing this place has a name, Bellevue, I mean... Langnac was pretty easy to find but then I had no idea how I would find Bellevue. So I asked at the garage just off the square and they gave me great directions. Well, the man made me a map...as I couldn't understand a word he said! I was just hoping there wasn't more than one

Bellevue. Wow!" he said, turning around, "It really is beautiful here."

By this time Clare had come out of the house and I introduced her to John and all the chatter in the court-yard brought Jean from his house and into our little group.

"Jean, this is my friend from the U.S., John! He has come and surprised us!"

"*Enchanté*, John! And how was your journey? Were you able to easily find the train at the airport in Paris?" Jean queried. I of course hadn't thought to ask, so surprised I was by seeing him here.

John responded by telling Jean "I met a Frenchman named Henri on the airplane, who was also headed to Bordeaux and he showed me exactly where to go, how to buy a train ticket and where to board the train. So I had had no trouble at all because of the kindness of a stranger."

Apparently John had had a good nap on the train and Henri had wakened him when it was time to leave the train in Bordeaux. The two of them had then walked to the Europcar rental office and found John a car and then Henri had marked up the map so John had driven right to Langnac as if he had known where he'd been going! He followed the signposts, finding one village then signposts for the next village's name and on and on... Then, without Henri, when he'd arrived in Langnac, John had stopped to ask directions and by some miracle understood them and driven right up the hill to our little piece of heaven!

"Jean, why don't you and Clare come up for an aperitif in a little while and in the meantime I will show John "my *pigeonnier.*" I suspect he would like a bit of rest after his journey and I'll get him settled. Clare, could you bring some crackers or something to munch on?"

And seeing Clare nod her OK I took John's hand and led him up to my September home.

As we walked through the door John stopped me. He put his arms around me and asked, "Marg, are you glad I came? Are you happy to see me?"

"I am just so surprised, John. I'm blown away that you came all this way!"

"You're not glad I came, are you?"

"Of course I am, John. Remember...you knew you were coming...I didn't... I am just shocked is all. Would you like something to eat or drink, or would you rather just lie down for a bit?"

"I could do with a glass of that good French wine, now that I'm not driving any longer! Why don't you have some too and tell me all about this disappearance you've been talking about. Is that Jean the guy who went missing? He looks like a nice enough fellow. What did you say he was doing in Paris?"

I went to the fridge and got a bottle of Cotes du Duras from the door, extricated the cork and poured John a glass.

"Yes, that is the guy. He went to Paris to take a small, but what has turned out to be a quite valuable, painting to a friend of his to assess."

And I told John the rest of the tale as I took some cheese out of the fridge and cut it into bite sized pieces and put it on a plate.

I looked up at John when he hadn't made a comment for a while and his eyes were closed. He was sound asleep, sitting upright in the chair! I had no clue how much of the story he had heard...

Linda Conn Amstutz

Chapter THIRTY-FOUR

September 1995, the hour of the aperitif

Bellevue

Clare rapped on the window and said it was just too lovely an evening to be indoors, we should all sit at the stone table overlooking the valley, so I should bring the wine, glasses, cheese and John and come to meet her and Jean there.

"John is sound asleep... I'll try to wake him."

A few minutes later the four of us met at the appointed place and sat. Clare had prepared a plate of melon and apricots with bits of sausage and brought a basket of thin slices of *baguette* - in short, a feast that might just take the place of supper, especially for poor, tired John.

He'd actually perked up a little since his nap. "Clare, this is just lovely and I'm grateful because I am really hungry, thanks." John gave her a warm smile.

"*Pas de problème*, John. We're happy to see you. We've heard so much about you and really didn't expect to be able to actually meet you."

"Well, I'm glad to meet you too. Marg's been keeping me informed about all the excitement that's been going on around here. Where is this fabulous painting anyhow?"

Jean answered, "It is in the safekeeping of my friend in Paris. He has been dealing all his life in art and he will keep it until we decide what is to be done with it. I suspect it may be sold at auction, at least that is what my friend Michel thinks is the best thing."

"Marg told me that you were involved with the resistance when you were very young," John ventured.

"Yes, our fathers were helping others to escape the Germans and it fell to Yves, Thierry and me on some occasions to do little jobs to also help: carry messages, stand as a lookout and so forth. Thierry was the one who was most involved. It was he who came upon the young Jewish girl and ended up taking this small treasure that her papa had given her to exchange it so she would have some money with her as she made her way to Spain with the help of our papas and some of their friends. We all did what we could to help."

John looked off into the distance and I imagined he was thinking what I had thought so many times sitting in this place looking over these gently rolling hills. He was trying to imagine how it felt to be invaded by a foreign army, to have shooting a constant threat and pillaging of your carefully put-by stores by a powerful force over which you had no control.

Then he said to no one in particular, "Just where were the Germans? Were they near here?"

Jean gestured away from the sunset. "Do you see that lane just beside my house? The other side of it was 'Occupied France' and this side was 'Free France' and there were checkpoints every few kilometres. One was between here and the village of Langnac and another just at the top of that rise there in the distance."

"Did you have no weapons? Wasn't there anything you could do to stop them, to force them away from your home? Did anyone even try?" John asked.

We looked at him and suddenly I began to understand the prejudice I had seen at home about the French during that war. John had put it into so few words, but he'd voiced the question those of us who'd never had an invading army in our backyard (in this case literally) find it so hard to understand.

Jean did his best to explain to John how his father and his father's friends had worked against the Germans in the dark, in secret, and how both Thierry's papa and his uncle had been killed, and how desperately difficult life became for their widows, how Thierry and his brother had literally taken the responsibility of his family's farm and his uncle's orchards working alongside his mother and his aunt, and how their private stories had been replicated all over France.

Jean told us how his own father had continued to organize the escapes of others even after his dear friend had been killed and how frightened his mother had become. He paused and gazed into the middle distance as he mentally returned to those years.

"One afternoon," he recalled, "Yves and I were stopped by the German soldiers at the checkpoint on the way to Langnac and they made us stand there for what seemed a very long time, with no explanation, then just let us go through to Yves' house in the village. The soldiers had that power and used it at every opportunity.

"We had little to eat and my *maman* managed by gathering the topinambour roots from our garden (which the Germans wouldn't eat)."

John interrupted, " What's topin...whatever he said?"

"We call them Jerusalem artichokes, John." Clare replied. "Plus they gathered mushrooms and chestnuts from the woods and if they kept chickens they had to hide them inside the barn. Jean and his friends and family had experienced deprivation that even hearing his stories, we could never know – and, actually wasn't that a good thing?"

Jean talked on as the sun went down and as we fetched another bottle of wine from Clare's cellar and finally, sitting there in the light of the single candle Clare had brought along with the second bottle of wine, in this place of peace and quiet beauty John quietly said, "I am sorry Jean, I simply had no idea."

Chapter THIRTY-FIVE

September 1995, Sunrise

The *Pigeonnier*, Bellevue

Margaret

At dawn, still, I lay awake as I had most of the night, thinking of what must be done yet reluctant to begin the process. I truly liked John and I admired him and knew he might be the most stable influence as a partner I would ever find. Stability would be a good thing in my life. These past twenty years as the owner of Concepts, Inc. had been a real roller coaster ride. Times were good, times were bad. I'd had enough workers to get my customers' jobs completed on time or there were too many - not enough work and someone had to be laid off. I really hated playing with peoples' lives like that...but those hard decisions are what kept us going for as long as we have been. A couple of times my own savings had to be emptied for us all to stay afloat.

But there were great times too: big contracts, happy customers, recognition of our contributions to our community - you just never knew what each year in business would bring.

Then there were the men I'd had been involved with: again, some were good, some not so good. I'd seen my life settling down as I let this relationship develop...how does anyone know who "the right one" is? Is there a "right one"?

Could I be a preacher's wife? What if John weren't so in love with me? Would I care enough for him to bridge the gap that eventuality would bring? Most men I've known I'd describe as mercurial creatures and when they're not driven by their hormones in your direction they're remarkably hard to predict. Would John be like that when his ardor cooled? And it would cool. I'm old enough and wise enough to know that much.

Another thing I know with certainty - he came here to ask the question.

Would I marry him?

What would I say?

I needed to get this thought-through before he awakened. I'd better know what I wanted to do, for if I hesitated, he would take advantage. I was sure of that. If he saw that I was not certain, he'd push for the answer he wanted. Then how strong would I be in the face of his perseverance? He was a kind man but he'd had lots of experience with people and he knew how to influence them to answer the way he wanted.

Why had he come to France? He came to seal this deal before I found something else I might want to do with my newly found freedom. I really didn't know what I would do after the business was sold, but I didn't want his ready made answer either. I wanted to find my own.

I didn't want to hurt him, and saying "no" would surely hurt him, but I really wasn't ready to get married. Too much was changing just then.

And this wasn't about Yves - not in the least.

John was stirring in the twin bed next to me - the bed where he fell instantly asleep after our makeshift picnic last evening and his nearly twenty-four-hour-long journey.

I decided to get up as silently as I could and go downstairs to find something substantial to cook for him for breakfast... Giving us something to talk about (in France you always talk about the food...) as well as some sustenance for what inevitably would be a long conversation later.

There was multi-fruit nectar in a liter bottle in the fridge. I'd make some good strong French drip coffee and warm the milk. I'd light the oven and warm up and freshen a couple buttery, flaky croissants from the freezer and then sauté a couple of eggs that I got from the farmer's wife halfway down the big hill. That ought to fortify us to choose a path either together or separately for the rest of our lives.

Perhaps I had made too much of this. I could have been wrong... Maybe he really did just need a break and missed me and came to see what it was that had drawn me here so many times...

Tap, tap, tap!

Clare opened the glass paned front door and whispered, "Good morning, is the traveler still asleep?"

Nodding my head and putting a finger to my lips to silence any further inquiry, I poured two mugs of coffee and added milk to both and sugar to mine and waved my hand for her to go back outside so we didn't hasten his awakening. Then, mugs in hand, I followed her out.

"I don't want to wake him," I said.

My intuitive old friend looked hard at me and asked, "Did he ask what he came to ask?"

I answered, as we walked down the lane toward the mailbox, "No."

"What will you say?"

"I'm not sure."

"Aren't you? He's a keeper, Marg. Don't be hasty."

She stopped in front of Jean's house and turned to look at me full on.

"Yeah, but I just hate to hurt him. He really is such a sweet guy and is vulnerable since his wife died, and I feel like I ought to have another alternative to say to him, 'No, John, I can't marry you...because...here is what I am going to do...'. And I don't...I don't have a clue what I am going to do when I don't have to go to work every day!" I sighed. "And, of course he's going to say, 'Then just marry me and we will work it out together'."

"Then, why don't you? Marry him and work it out together, I mean?"

"Because I want to work it out myself, alone. There, I said it! I have been doing what someone else wanted or needed for the last twenty years and it hasn't been bad. I don't mean that, but I need some time and some space and as tempting as the security of marriage is, I just don't want it. He's a lovely man, but he couldn't even 'get' that I wanted to come here and just 'be here' for a month... He had to come clear across the Atlantic to...to see why I sounded strange on the phone."

"Ok, I get it" said my sweet, understanding friend.

Clare walked past Jean's to the mailbox and pulled a letter from the back pocket of her jeans. She stuck it in the door so it protruded just a little (so the postman would know to stop), then took my arm and walked me silently back to my pigeonnier, kissed me on the cheek, patted me on the shoulder and walked home.

Linda Conn Amstutz

Chapter THIRTY-SIX

September 9, 1995

Aravell, Spain (in Catalonia above the valley of the Rio Segre)

The silver-haired woman sat gazing wistfully over the orchards and beyond them the mountains, so familiar and so lovely in the warm morning's sunlight. She took another sip of the creamy coffee which had long been as cool as the air was and looked again at the newspaper on the tiny round ironwork table on her balcony.

Langnac. How long had it been since she had thought the name of that town?

Langnac... Cold. Langnac... Hungry. Langnac... Fear. Langnac... Kindness. Langnac.

She rubbed her swollen inflamed knuckles, gnarled beyond any likeness to the pretty and slender hands of her youth. Of course, she didn't want to – but it had been years since she could – remove the precious thin gold band on her left hand.

Her slender silver braid that had once been so thick and wavy was now twisted and pinned at the nape of her neck. It bore little resemblance to the rich dark tresses that had once beguiled Raoul. She looked out over her farm (hers now that Raoul was gone) which was also different from the urban life she'd led as a child in Liège.

How her life had changed in the village of Langnac, France! Her eyelids closed, and she recalled now the night the man had died.

His wife with the kind eyes, swollen from tears, had come into the barn and given her the dead man's coat for her journey through the mountains. "He will no longer need it," she had said, "and you surely will." The poor woman had held her in such a fierce embrace and muttered words into her hair that must have been prayers – for what or whom she couldn't discern. She wished she could have seen the boy, Thierry, but he had not come into the barn again.

Awash in the memory, she felt again the frisson of terror when yet another stranger, a sturdy-built man, had led her from the barn that she had come to see as her refuge and into the chill of that moonlit night.

She had silently followed him. Or course she hadn't known his name. She was wearing the clothes of the man who had died, at least the coat was his... They were heavy and rather too large for her but the night was frosty and soon she was grateful for the warmth they afforded her.

No one had spoken.

They walked on trails through the woods for what seemed hours and hours. Soon they began to climb, the path became rocky. Annaliesa stumbled, and the man hesitated for a moment then told her, hissing urgently, that she must keep up. They had no time to waste so she tried to go faster. It was difficult and it was very cold.

It got harder.

Just about dawn they met another man on the trail. He was younger and small built. The first stranger turned back toward the place from which they had come. In a few minutes they heard shouting, German shouting, then gunfire. The younger man grabbed Annaliesa and all but carried her into the deeper part of the woods where they lay under some thick foliage. She was afraid even to breathe. A very long time passed and the sounds of the German patrol ebbed away, apparently satisfied that the man they had shot was alone. Annaliesa and the small man waited longer.

The sun was high in the sky when they finally came out from beneath the thicket and after moving the dead man's body off the trail they cautiously continued their journey. The man had some bread and ham in a satchel and shared it with Annaliesa. She ate like a starving dog! Her feet hurt and as they continued to climb she became short of breath and cold, very cold.

And still they walked.

As the light failed that second day they came to a rough shelter - not a cabin, really, more like a lean-to for animals. They stopped there and ate some more of the bread and ham. Annaliesa had prayed they could stop as she didn't think she could walk any more and her prayer was answered, at least for a while.

When the moon rose the duo were off again scrambling over rocks and down gullies. Now it seemed they were going more down than up and it was even more difficult footing.

Annaliesa walked and walked, thinking each time she couldn't take another step, but she did because he kept going and while the walking was so hard, the thought of being left alone there in the mountains was more frightening. She was so grateful to the man who had died trying to take her to safety, no, she couldn't stop, no matter how tired she was.

Finally, after two more days of this madness, her companion said this was "it". This was the border of Spain.

Annaliesa asked, "I am safe now?"

The man replied that she would still need to remain hidden as there were Germans around and those who were helping her would be in jeopardy if it were discovered that they were harbouring a Jewish child.

Was she never to feel safe? How would her parents ever find her here in this remote place?

Even in the relative safety of Spain she was kept in hiding and moved from place to place in the night. Always it was by people she had not seen before and whose names she never learned.

She closed her watery eyes and recalled Raoul's mother and her sweet nature. How she had climbed the stairs every day bringing her food, combing her hair, providing her with clothing and bedding and carrying away her waste. For nearly two years she was kept in hiding in that attic room. She could see light through the louvered opening, but not the sun or the rolling countryside. The only company she had were Raoul's mother and of course Raoul. During his daily visits he had taught her his Catalan language.

When finally she was able go out, she learned how to be helpful in the orchards where they grew apricots and olives. She became almost a member of the family. Raoul's sweet concern for her shortened the days and eased her worry about her parents. At least it was eased for a while, until the Frenchmen returned, having delivered other refugees, and she had heard their hushed voices talking in the room below about the places they took the Jews in Germany. The things they did.

The millions of people who died.

The millions.

Probably her parents were gone, and she could only hope their deaths had been swift and painless but the stories she heard gave her grave doubts.

Raoul knew her fears, he listened to her stories of Liège and her tutor and her parents and her friends whom, by now, she had no hope of ever seeing again. He was sympathetic and kind, and then something more - he wanted her to stay. He wanted her to give up hope of ever going back.

"Marry me, Annaliesa, and stay in this place. We can have a good life here. It isn't the life you would have had in Liège, but I can promise you love and also good work to fill our days together." He wanted her to share this peaceful and comfortable life of hard work and strong family ties in Catalonia. She felt, at sixteen, she had no future, no hope beyond this small Catalan farm. The wide world which had once provided her hope had shrunk to this small sweet place.

And Raoul.

Their life together had been good. It had been productive and simple and rich in love and, of course, he had been right about the work! Their daughter had been the light of her father's life and of hers.

Now, today, as Annaliesa was lost in thoughts of Langnac, Eleana climbed the stairs to the balcony where her mother sat and quietly asked where her tears came from.

"It is a story in the newspaper here," she gestured to the table.

"The village in France where I was hidden for a while is here in this article. They have, in the church there, put a wonderful organ which was made in the United States, carried to France and installed. It actually belongs to a wealthy local man who lives in the chateau in the town. He loves to play the organ but thought it selfish to have such a fine instrument only for his pleasure, so he had it put in the small and very old church in the village. They write about it here be-cause it was such an unselfish act and so unusual to have an American pipe organ in so small a place.

"I wonder sometimes about the people I knew there." She looked at her daughter. "They must be old now too. Perhaps the kind woman is gone as your Grandmama is. And the boy who helped me - he will be an old man as I am an old woman. His friend's fa-ther was the sacristain of that church - the same one where they put the new organ. That war was so long ago. Perhaps the tiny painting my papa gave me is still there in that town, maybe in the church, or perhaps in the chateau of the man who bought the organ. The money for the painting had to have come from some-where. I have often wondered."

Eleana took her mother's hands in hers and looked into her eyes, thinking about the stories she had heard from both her parents and how these things had changed their lives.

"Would you like to go there once more to see this place again and perhaps find the people who risked so much for you? It would be good to do it sooner rather than later - as you and they are not getting younger! I would like to help you do this if you want to go. Would you?" Eleana asked her mother.

"Perhaps, Eleana, perhaps...but only if I don't have to walk!"

And they both giggled and all the sadness Annaliesa had felt was washed away by the sound of her daughter's laughter.

Acknowledgements

This book is the product of several years toil. Authors, despite the popular image of a hermit-like creature pecking away at a computer or scribbling in an attic room, are, if they are lucky, surrounded by encouragement and assistance.

My friend Richard Savin, an author himself, (most recently - <u>More than One Passion</u>) actually convinced me this book had merit, that I should finish it and share it with you! Thanks also must go to Ted Bun, author of <u>Runners and Riders</u>. One of my favorite mystery writers gave me very valuable advice, many thanks to Marsali Taylor, author of the Shetland Sailing Mysteries.

It needed a fine tuned eye which it got from painstakingly tenacious editor and friend Stephanie Patterson, an author herself (<u>Love Lost in Time.</u>)

Members of my writing group in Medina, Ohio, Jane Snow, Ann Sheldon Mezger, Gloria Brown and Nancy

Heslop who showed such patience in the early days are due a debt of gratitude.

The cover art was a labor of love by the ever forbearing Lindy Nobles - long distance from Prosper TX and she worked with the perfect front cover photograph by Debbra Obertanec of Shadetree Photography.

To say this was a community effort would be an understatement. My most sincere thanks to you all!

Last but surely not least, thanks are due to the late Tony Roberts, who sitting next to an older unnamed Frenchman in a bar over thirty years ago, listened to, and then related to me, the story of the old man's childhood as a messenger for the Maquis during WWII... so at least that part of this tale is true.

About the Author

Linda Conn Amstutz has been writing all her life, first for herself, then as a single handed sailor for newspapers and magazines and now with her first novel, "The Bicycle Messenger."

She lived in Northern Ohio for most of her life, then moved to her precious boat "Modachaidh" on the US east coast.

Now, settled in her centuries old stone house in the south of France with her dog, Maggie and two cats, Paddy and Mary, we may expect many more stories!

"The Bicycle Messenger" is a work of historical fiction set in Linda's beloved France both in 1995 and 1941.

Join her on Facebook and/or see her blog at lindaconnamstutz.wordpress.com

---

* * * *

Made in the USA
Monee, IL
04 October 2020